"Wha
of, Miss Copeland?

His question surprised her. He had the
disconcerting habit of moving the conversation in
unexpected directions, never quite following things
along a straight line.

Davidian leaned forward with his elbows on the
desk and laced his long brown fingers under his
chin.

"I don't know what you mean," she answered,
frowning.

"Don't you?" His tone implied that he didn't believe
her. He fixed her with another penetrating stare.
"You say your partner walked out on you. So why
don't you get on with running the business
yourself? Sitting around sniveling, my dear Miss
Copeland, never got anybody anywhere."

Sniveling? How dared he? Indignation kept
Giselle speechless.

Stephanie Howard is a British author whose two ambitions since childhood were to see the world and write. Her first venture into the world was a four-year stay in Italy, learning the language and supporting herself by writing short stories. Then her sensible side brought her back to London to read Social Administrations at the London School of Economics. She has held various editorial posts at magazines such as *Reader's Digest*, *Vanity Fair*, *Women's Own*, as well as writing free-lance for *Cosmopolitan*, *Good Housekeeping* and *the Observer*.

Books by Stephanie Howard

HARLEQUIN ROMANCE
3093—MASTER OF GLEN CRANNACH

HARLEQUIN PRESENTS
1098—RELUCTANT PRISONER
1130—DARK LUCIFER
1168—HIGHLAND TURMOIL
1273—BRIDE FOR A PRICE
1307—KISS OF THE FALCON

Don't miss any of our special offers. Write to us at the following address for information on our newest releases.

Harlequin Reader Service
P.O. Box 1397, Buffalo, NY 14240
Canadian address: P.O. Box 603,
Fort Erie, Ont. L2A 5X3

AN IMPOSSIBLE PASSION

Stephanie Howard

Harlequin Books

TORONTO • NEW YORK • LONDON
AMSTERDAM • PARIS • SYDNEY • HAMBURG
STOCKHOLM • ATHENS • TOKYO • MILAN

Original hardcover edition published in 1990
by Mills & Boon Limited

ISBN 0-373-03112-2

Harlequin Romance first edition March 1991

AN IMPOSSIBLE PASSION

CHAPTER ONE

IT WAS a good three-mile hike from the spot where the little country bus had dropped her off to the imposing gates of Chiltham Hall, and Giselle was feeling decidedly footsore as she jammed her finger against the brass bell. She scowled and shook back her mane of Titian hair. On top of all her other woes, a pair of blistered, aching feet was the very last thing she needed now!

After a pause came a crackle on the entryphone grille. 'Hello. Who's there?' enquired a polite female voice.

Giselle leaned towards the grille to answer the disembodied voice. 'It's Miss Copeland to see Mr Davidian,' she explained. 'I'm from Silver Service Catering.' Even as she spoke the name, she felt a bitter inward wrench. To all intents and purposes, Silver Service Catering was now defunct, which was precisely the reason she was here.

She waited, straightening the skirt of her neat blue suit and adjusting the collar of her pale cream shirt, as there followed another, slightly shorter pause before the big gates finally buzzed open.

'Come in,' the woman's voice instructed.

Already Giselle was bracing herself for another considerable hike. The stately eighteenth-century mansion known as Chiltham Hall stood well back from the narrow country road, behind a lush, protective screen of trees. And the wide, sweeping driveway followed a gentle incline for at least a quarter of a mile before opening out on to a vast gravel forecourt with stunning views out over the grounds.

Giselle paused to glance at neither the stunning views nor the imposing façade of the old country house as she reached the forecourt at last and strode purposefully towards the wide stone steps that led up to the huge front door. She had not come on some sightseeing tour, but on an errand that personally grieved her and which she wished to accomplish with all possible speed.

Besides which, she was thinking with an edge of bitterness, a leisurely appreciation of the riches that fate chose to shower upon her fellow men, such as the mysterious Fayiz Davidian, was not something she had much of a stomach for these days. Not while she was still mentally reeling from the cruelly ungenerous blow that she herself had so recently been dealt.

A woman in a blue-checked housekeeper's uniform was waiting in the open doorway. Round eyes in a chubby, kindly face regarded Giselle with mild concern. 'My dear, I'd no idea you were on foot! I'd have sent someone down to the gates to pick you up if I'd known you were without a car.'

With an effort, Giselle suppressed a grimace. Her lack of transport was a very sore point—in more ways than one, she thought ironically, glancing downwards at her feet. She threw the woman a grateful smile. 'That's OK,' she reassured her. 'It's quite a pleasant little walk up the drive.' Or it might have been, she added wryly to herself, if she hadn't already had to hike the three miles from the bus as well!

The woman was leading her across a marble-tiled hall, strewn in colourful abandon with silk Persian rugs. 'I gather Mr Davidian wasn't expecting you, and he's rather tied up at the moment,' she explained. She showed her young guest into a small reception room, richly furnished, and bade her sit down. 'However, he's promised he'll see you just as soon as he gets off the phone.' She smiled again, sympathetically. 'I hope you don't mind waiting for a bit?'

Just for a moment, Giselle was tempted to take advantage of this opening, plead some pressing engagement and entreat the kindly housekeeper to relay in her stead the bad news she had brought. It would save her the embarrassment, and possibly the hassle, of having to face Mr Davidian herself. If he was as abrupt and abrasive in person as she remembered him being over the phone, though not quite honourable, such a move might prove wise. She was in no frame of mind at the moment for confrontations of any kind.

But already the woman was taking her leave. She hovered for a moment in the doorway. 'I'll bring you some tea while you're waiting—or would you prefer coffee?' she offered.

Giselle smiled back politely. 'Thank you. Tea would be fine.' Then, left alone in the room, she glanced round idly at her surroundings and wondered about the man she had come to see.

She knew little about Fayiz Davidian beyond the indisputable fact that he was a man who preferred to keep himself to himself. An immensely wealthy Lebanese with his own private investment corporation in the City, he had acquired historic Chiltham Hall, here in the heart of rural Kent, just over a year ago. A weekend retreat from the hurly-burly of London, according to the stories she had heard—though if this was merely a weekend retreat, she found herself wondering with some awe what his principal residence in the capital must be like!

The thought sent a stab of resentment through her. It was all right for some! Some had riches handed to them on a plate, while others, like herself, no matter how hard they toiled, seemed destined to end up with not a penny to their name.

On a wave of frustration, she got to her feet and crossed impatiently to the window, fists thrust into the pockets of her jacket, a frown darkening her flawless, ivory-skinned face. It wasn't fair, she reflected bitterly, tossing back her red-gold hair, as she stared with unseeing gold-flecked eyes at the glorious landscape that stretched outside. Savagely, she bit at her lower lip as tears of self-pity pricked her eyes. Life just wasn't fair at all!

Behind her, suddenly, a door clicked open and a figure stepped into the room.

Hearing the click, Giselle took a deep breath, blinked back her tears and pinned on a smile. Then, once more composed, she turned around, expecting to see the housekeeper with her tea. But it was not the homely figure of the housekeeper, but a very different sight that met her eyes.

A man in a sharply cut dark suit, white shirt, blue tie. Tall, black-haired and unsmiling, with an indefinable aura about him—a kind of magnetic authority and power—that sent a shiver of uneasiness whispering down her spine.

'Miss Copeland?' a rich, deep voice enquired. 'You wish to see me, I understand?'

'Yes.' As she nodded, he came towards her and the uneasiness in her increased. He moved with the grace and power of a panther and with the same unhurried, purposeful stride. And the coal-black eyes with their thick fringe of lashes regarded her with the same detachment that a panther might regard a stray gazelle. Beware should I grow hungry! they warned.

His handshake was brief but firm—strong, lean fingers grasping hers for no more than a fraction of a second. But, as she dropped her hand to her side, her nerve-ends were tingling strangely. Her eyes followed the movements of his well-shaped lips as he informed her curtly, 'Fayiz Davidian'. Then he was turning abruptly and leading her towards the doorway at the end of the room, from which he had emerged.

Beyond was a remarkably well-equipped study, a replica of a high-powered City office, complete with a desk the size of a billiard table and a baffling battery of monitors and phones.

Giselle glanced askance at the dark, remote

figure as he lowered his sinuously muscular frame into the swivel chair behind the huge desk and bade her, with a gesture, to take a seat. It was a warm and sunny Sunday afternoon in the middle of May and the rest of the world was enjoying a day off, whereas here, in his luxurious weekend retreat, it was evidently business as usual for Fayiz Davidian.

He leaned back in the high-backed chair and regarded her through narrowed black eyes, the strong-boned features of his face politely impassive as he enquired, 'I take it you wish to see me about the dinner I've hired you for next Tuesday?'

Awkwardly, Giselle cleared her throat. Instinctively she knew that her task, already quite painful enough, was about to be made even more difficult by the man on the other side of the desk. She said apologetically, clasping her hands tightly in her lap and crossing her slim legs at the ankles, 'I tried to phone you several times this morning, not to mention several times yesterday as well, but your number was constantly engaged . . .'

'Yes, I have been rather busy this weekend.' He allowed himself a brief, tolerant smile, then raised one curved black eyebrow at her, inviting her to carry on.

'So I thought I'd better come round personally and explain the situation to you.' As she nervously circled round the point she was inwardly bracing herself to make, she was aware of the sharp lines of impatience that now etched the corners of the wide, masculine mouth. An impatience that was echoed within herself. It wasn't like her to procrastinate like this. She took a deep breath and plunged straight in. 'This dinner on Tuesday, Mr Davidian. I'm afraid I'm going to have to cancel it,' she said.

The dark eyes turned to a pair of cinders. 'I'm afraid you can't,' was his crushing response.

Giselle's nails were digging into her palms. So he was, after all, as abrupt in person as she recalled him being over the phone! But she wasn't about to let his abrasive and overbearing manner put her off. She took a deep breath and continued politely, 'I'm afraid I have no choice. You see, Silver Service Catering is no more.'

Fayiz Davidian appeared not to hear. His tone was cut glass as he told her, 'I'm really not interested in your personal problems. I have contracted you and your company to provide dinner for twelve on Tuesday evening, and that, my dear Miss Copeland, is precisely what I shall expect you to do.'

'I'm sorry, you don't understand. I'm no longer in a position to honour the contract.' Her voice wavered dangerously as she added, 'I've just lost my partner. She walked out on me.'

She had been half expecting—or at least, hoping—that this miserable revelation might soften his heart. Surely no one could help but feel sympathy for one who had suffered such a treacherous blow.

No one save Fayiz Davidian, it seemed. Without

the faintest suspicion of a softened heart, he leaned towards her across the desk, the olive-gold skin of his strongly-boned hands a striking contrast against the snowy-white shirt cuffs. 'Which leaves you in command,' he observed, cynically matter-of-fact. The dark eyes bored without compassion into hers. 'You should be grateful to your defecting partner, Miss Copeland. Sharing power tends to be an unsatisfactory business. It is always preferable to be in sole command.'

An image of the solitary panther, stalking his terrain alone, flashed vividly across Giselle's brain. Total command, undivided power, those were the ideals this man would adhere to. She felt a shiver run through her as she met the ruthless dark gaze. He would give no quarter; and expect none in return.

As he continued to watch her, she straightened in her seat. 'I'm afraid you still don't understand. When my partner, Joanne, walked out, she demanded her share of the business in cash.' Joanne's original input had been her own money, a present from her parents, whereas Giselle had taken out a loan from the bank. A loan that she now feared she would have considerable difficulty in paying back.

Her tone laced with self-pity, she told Davidian, 'We had to sell the van and most of the more expensive equipment so that Joanne could have the money the partnership owed her, and I've been left with a considerable debt.'

Again, if she had expected sympathy, Fayiz

Davidian offered her not one gramme. Instead he observed with a lift of one eyebrow, 'Let that be a lesson to you. One should never go into partnership with a woman. As you have discovered for yourself, they are a singularly faithless and untrustworthy breed.'

At the insult, Giselle bridled. Perhaps it had escaped his notice that she herself was a member of that breed! Her gold-flecked eyes flashed accusingly across at him. 'Surely that's an unnecessarily chauvinistic remark!'

He leaned back in his chair and folded his arms across his chest. 'You may call it chauvinistic, Miss Copeland. I prefer to call it deductive. Culled from my own not inconsiderable personal experience over the years.'

Through her irritation, Giselle found herself studying the uncompromising details of his face—that boldly defined nose, as cruel as a hawk's, the steel-trap mouth, the firm chin and jaw, and, most of all, the laser-like eyes beneath the intelligent dark curve of his brow. Experience, he had said. Yes, she could read experience in that face. A breadth of experience, she sensed, that surpassed the simple experience of years. He would be about thirty-four years old, a decade older than herself, yet far more than a decade separated them in their respective experiences of life.

He was watching her with equal interest, as unfolding his arms now, he enquired, 'So, what caused this unreliable partner of yours to walk out and leave you in the lurch?'

Giselle regarded him narrowly, still resenting that uncalled-for slur. 'A man,' she informed him tartly, adding rhetorically, 'What else?'

The fleeting hint of a smile touched his lips. She caught a flash of strong white teeth. 'I see,' he answered slowly. 'It was fickle love that lured her away.'

More fickle than he could possibly imagine, Giselle acknowledged dully to herself. For the unpalatable truth of the matter was that the man her friend and partner, Joanne, had left her in the lurch to run off with was the same man Giselle had once thought of as hers. She saw no need, however, to share this additional humiliation with Davidian. In a controlled and even voice, she explained, 'It was really all rather sudden. That's why I still haven't quite found my feet. And why,' she added, returning to the point, 'I'm having to cancel all standing bookings—including yours, I'm afraid. However,' she hurried to reassure him, catching the dangerous glint in his eyes, 'I'd be more than happy to recommend a couple of other excellent caterers who I'm sure could provide you with what you need.'

He regarded her coldly. 'At such short notice? I find that a little hard to believe.'

He had a point, Giselle acknowledged silently. Tuesday was only two days away and a dinner for twelve was no mean undertaking. But she pressed on, determined to convince him. 'If you like, I'll have a word with them on your behalf. I'm sure we can come to some satisfactory arrangement.'

Davidian leaned forward with his elbows on the desk and laced his long brown fingers under his chin. He regarded her contemplatively for a moment, then took her totally by surprise. 'What are you so afraid of, Miss Copeland?' he enquired.

He had this disorientating habit of moving the conversation in unexpected directions, never quite following things on in a straight line. Giselle looked back at him uneasily. 'I don't know what you mean,' she answered, frowning.

'Don't you?' His tone implied he did not believe her. He fixed her with another penetrating stare. 'You say your partner's walked out on you . . . So why don't you just stop wallowing in self-pity and get on with running the business yourself? Sitting around snivelling, my dear Miss Copeland, never got anybody anywhere.'

His words rubbed like sandpaper against Giselle's nerves. Snivelling? How dared he? Wallowing in self-pity? The unutterable nerve! She straightened and shot him a withering look that would have demolished a lesser man.

'I've already told you, Mr Davidian, I have no money, very little equipment and no means of transport at all. How am I supposed to get on with running my business when I no longer have the tools?' Or the heart, she added to herself, but refrained from expressing the sentiment out loud. Her shattered state of mind would not concern him. The milk of human sympathy evidently ran somewhat thinly in those unforgiving veins.

He shrugged. 'So what do you intend to do? Sit weeping forlornly in a corner—or go running off home with your tail between your legs to let Mummy and Daddy look after you?'

The latter thought had never even crossed her mind—though she knew that her parents back in Hereford would have welcomed her with open arms. She glared indignantly across at him. 'No, I don't, as a matter of fact.'

'No doubt, in that case, you have a boyfriend you can count on to pay your bills for you.' His tone of voice was pure knife-edged scorn as he added before she had time to butt in, 'That, of course, as we all know, is always a favourite female ploy.'

'Not of mine, it isn't!' She was a young woman who had always prided herself fiercely on her total financial independence and the gross unfairness of Davidian's remark brought a flush of righteous anger to Giselle's fair-skinned cheeks. The man was clearly a misogynist—this was *at least* his second anti-female remark within the space of a few minutes—but he had no right to apply his prejudices to her. Absolutely no right at all! Belligerently, she shook back her red-gold hair and opened her mouth to tell him so.

But opening her mouth was as far as she got. The study door opened with a click and the housekeeper in the blue-checked uniform came into the room, carrying a tray.

'Ah, Mrs Pennygreen. What a pleasant surprise!' A rare smile parted Davidian's lips as the woman crossed the silent carpet to lay the tray down on the desk.

'I hope I'm not interrupting, Mr Davidian, but I promised the young lady a cup of tea.' She threw a kindly smile in Giselle's direction, as she laid out a single teacup and saucer with an individual teapot, plus sugar and milk. She glanced across at Davidian again. 'And I brought coffee for you, sir,' she added, arranging before him a Turkish coffee-pot, a cup and saucer and a glass of water. 'I thought you might be ready for one.'

'You thought right.' Again the warm flash of a smile that momentarily transformed the harsh lines of his face. So after all, Giselle pondered, as she politely nodded her thanks to the woman, he was capable of civility towards the female sex. But then Mrs Pennygreen was a mere servant. A woman who, servant-like, knew her place.

As Mrs Pennygreen retreated, the dark eyes fixed on Giselle once more. 'So. I believe you were about to tell me what it is that you intend to do?'

'On the contrary, I was about to tell you that it's none of your damned business!'

'Ah, but it is.' In one fluid movement, he raised the brass coffee-pot and emptied the aromatic contents into his cup. 'It is very much my damned business when you come here telling me, forty-eight hours before the event, that you intend welching on our contract.' He laid down the coffee-pot and fixed her with a stony stare. 'Only after, I may point out, you have already cashed my advance deposit cheque.'

Instantly Giselle was fumbling for her bag,

fiery-faced with sudden embarrassment. How could she have been so unwary as to allow such a thing to slip her mind? How could she have let him believe that she had even the remotest intention of cheating him? Hurriedly she extricated from her wallet the refund cheque she had written in advance. 'I'm returning your deposit, Mr Davidian. Every single penny of it.' She thrust the evidence across the desk towards him. 'I think you'll find this quite in order.'

'You think so, do you?' He threw the cheque a contemptuous look and took a mouthful of his coffee, regarding her with equal contempt over the rim of his cup as he drank. Then, deliberately, he laid down the cup and took a mouthful of the water. The dark eyes never left her face. 'I'm afraid, Miss Copeland, I find nothing whatsoever about this transaction in order. You undertook to provide dinner next Tuesday for some very important clients of mine. In the world in which I operate, a contract is a contract and must be kept. I do not, as you call it, find it "in order" when somebody chooses to let me down.'

'It wasn't my choice. I've been let down too.'

'So you keep reminding me.' As he held her eyes, the words 'wallowing' and 'snivelling' trembled almost audibly in the air. But he didn't repeat them. Instead he reminded her, 'I've already told you that's not my problem.'

Giselle, with difficulty, held his eyes. 'Well, I'm sorry, but I've returned your deposit and I'm afraid that's the best that I can do.'

One strong-boned hand reached out towards the cheque and held it up for a moment between them. 'I'm sorry too, Miss Copeland,' he intoned, his entire demeanour subtly conveying the contempt in which he held the contentious piece of paper. 'But I have no use for your thoughtful refund.' To prove his point, with a curl of his lips he tore the cheque first in halves and then in quarters and tossed the mangled pieces disdainfully aside. 'What I have need of, and what I *demand*, is your presence in my kitchen on Tuesday night.'

Tight-lipped, she answered, 'Well, I'm sorry I can't help you.' *Demand*, indeed!

Fayiz Davidian leaned towards her, his jaw tightening ominously as he put to her, 'Are you always so cavalier about the commitments you make? No wonder you have no doting boyfriend eager to pay your bills for you.'

That was cruel. Crueller than he knew. She felt herself blanch, momentarily thrown, then, fatally, she rushed to defend herself. 'How can you possibly expect me to prepare and serve a four-course dinner for twelve people entirely on my own? It's perfectly ludicrous! It can't be done!'

He leaned back in his chair again and smiled the satisfied smile of a panther who knows that he has cornered his prey. 'Alas, Miss Copeland, I'm afraid it must.'

'And how am I supposed to get here with all the things I'm going to need? I've already told you I have no transport. And half of my equipment has been sold!'

'I can provide you with temporary transport. That particular problem is easily solved. As to the equipment you say you're missing, I'm sure you'll find everything you could possibly need in the kitchen here.'

Giselle looked across at him in helpless frustration. Somehow, without quite understanding how it had happened, she had walked into a trap she could see no way out of. 'I'd really prefer just to write you another cheque,' she protested feebly, knowing she was beaten. 'And I'd be more than happy to make alternative arrangements with some other caterers on your behalf.'

But her protests were a waste of breath. The discussion was about to be unilaterally terminated. Fayiz Davidian glanced at his watch. 'You've already wasted enough of my time, Miss Copeland. I'm a very busy man.' Deliberately, he began to rise to his feet. 'I shall send round a car to your address early tomorrow morning and you may have the use of it for a couple of days. For shopping, transporting things——' he waved an elegantly dismissive hand '—and whatever else you might need it for.'

Giselle sighed and started to stand up, then couldn't resist pointing out to him, 'Of course, you understand that in these far from ideal circumstances I can't possibly guarantee the standard of service we would normally provide.'

Suddenly he had come round to the front of the desk and was standing almost right on top of her. A firm hand closed around her elbow, ostensibly guiding her towards the door, yet the unyielding clasp of the cool, strong fingers conveyed a very different message.

His voice was a soft but threatening purr as he informed her in careful syllables, 'I shall expect the meal, Miss Copeland, to be served at eight-thirty on the dot, as we arranged. I shall likewise expect the menu to be that upon which we agreed earlier by phone. And furthermore, I shall expect the very highest standard of service—the standard to which my guests are accustomed and for which I happen to be paying.' He smiled down at her without a trace of humour. 'Miss Copeland, do I make myself clear?'

Abundantly! A shiver went through her from scalp to toes as she forced herself to meet his gaze, observing, quite incongruously, that the irises of the black-fringed eyes were so dark they were totally indistinguishable from the pupils in the centre. She had never seen such eyes before. Nor had she any wish to be quite so close to them at this moment.

She tried to tug her arm away, failed—and retaliated with defiance. 'I'll do my best,' she promised sarcastically.

Davidian did not respond warmly to sarcasm. His grip around her elbow tightened as he paused on their journey to the door. 'No, Miss Copeland, you will not do your best. You will do exactly as I say. Take my word for it, you would be wise indeed to ensure that the demands of this particular customer are fully and unconditionally met.'

And what was that supposed to mean? 'Is that some kind of threat?'

'Threat?' Black eyebrows soared in a show of denial, as though he found the very notion both deplorable and alien. 'Do I appear to you the sort of man who would issue threats, Miss Copeland?' he queried.

Yes. But she did not say it. She was far too conscious of his nearness and of the uncomfortable way it made her feel. Not threatened, exactly—at least, not in the sense that he might do her some injury. Despite the ruthless iron band that was digging into the flesh of her arm, Fayiz Davidian, she knew instinctively, was far too cultured and civilised a man to even dream of inflicting harm on a female. In spite of his low opinion of 'the breed'.

But the way he was standing over her, the broad torso almost brushing against her breasts, the clean male scent of him in her nostrils, was causing wild palpitations in her heart. All at once, the blood was rushing through her veins and her breath seemed to come in coarse, harsh pants. It was not a sensation she cared for in the least. A sudden emotional claustrophobia seemed to grip her.

And then he was moving even closer and every sinew in her body froze.

'After you, Miss Copeland. Please.'

But he had simply been leaning past her to open up the study door. Intense, irrational relief washed through her as he held it open for her now and urged her to pass ahead of him out into the hall. Still with that hand closed round her elbow, fingers burning through the fabric of her jacket, sending hot and cold shivers over her flesh.

'Until Tuesday, then. Feel free to install yourself in the kitchen whenever you please.' As they reached the front door, he paused to glance down at her. 'Be sure to give yourself all the time you need to have everything geared up for half past eight.' With that final dictate, he opened the front door and released her arm at last. 'Goodbye, Miss Copeland,' the deep voice purred. 'Till we meet again.'

Giselle neither answered nor turned around. Her arm was still tingling furiously as she hurried down the steps and her legs felt curiously unsteady and weak. Anger, she firmly reassured herself. Anger and frustration and indignation and rage.

For it struck her as she headed across the forecourt and down the driveway towards the road, on another long hike back the way she had come, that she'd just allowed herself to be roped into something that she should never have agreed to in a million years! Not that she had actually agreed, of course. The entire thing had been thrust upon her, as though her agreement in the matter were entirely superfluous!

'Damn you, Fayiz Davidian!' she muttered with feeling to herself. 'Maybe you're used to laying down the law, but I can still have the last laugh yet! What's to stop me simply failing to turn up on Tuesday night?'

A sudden flash of those fierce dark eyes and the feel of the hard fingers grasping her arm went

skittering across her brain. 'Damn you!' she
muttered again, but less forcefully, with an uneasy
shiver.

For, deep in her heart, she already knew that it
would take a braver soul than she to cross Fayiz
Davidian. Somehow, within the next forty-eight
hours, she must find a way to meet his
demands—or be prepared to pay the cost!

CHAPTER TWO

THERE was at least one positive outcome to the events of that Sunday afternoon. After her meeting with Fayiz Davidian, the woes that had previously been besetting Giselle melted like moonglow from her mind. An untrue friend, a faithless lover and a business on the point of demise were mere tiny pinpricks compared to him! At this man's ruthless hands, she sensed, she could soon discover what real hell was!

The first thing she had done when she'd got home, footsore and weary after her long walk, had been to look out the appropriate file and check up on Davidian's order. Since she appeared to have no choice but to deliver, she might as well see what she'd let herself in for. Though she had a nasty, sneaking suspicion that she remembered all too well.

She'd groaned as she read the details. She'd been absolutely right. For the delectation of his eleven guests Davidian had chosen the menu that Giselle and Joanne used jokingly to refer to as the 'Twenty-four-carat Super Deluxe'. Caviare, smoked salmon and quails, veal stuffed with truffles—the works! In the two years that Silver Service Catering had been in operation, they had been called upon to provide the Deluxe only a couple of times before, but Giselle could remember all too vividly the nightmare preparations it had entailed—and at that time there had been two of them doing the work!

She sank down in a chair, her head in her hands. Perhaps she ought seriously to consider skipping the country before Tuesday night!

At the thought, a familiar hurt welled up inside her. Skip the country. That's what *they'd* done—Ken and Joanne.

She sat up and sighed and stared into space, letting the pain of her betrayal wash over her. Of course, she had seen it coming, the sudden mad passion between her lover and her friend that had swept them both away from her. Hadn't she seen it in their eyes that very first time she'd brought Ken home to introduce him to her house-mate and partner?

But knowing, and fearing, what was to come hadn't made the fatal moment any easier when Ken had finally broken the news. He and Joanne were desperately in love and had been seeing one another secretly.

Giselle had smiled bravely, she remembered, and granted him his freedom with all the dignity she could muster. There had been no point in letting him see the hurt and disappointment that raged inside. 'I wish you both the best of luck,' she'd said, as though she meant it. 'Joanne's a super girl.'

He'd smiled lamely, evidently relieved. 'I hope that means we can still all be friends.'

'Of course we can still all be friends,' she had assured him, secretly dreading what that might entail. To be spurned for another was hurtful enough. To have to witness daily the humiliating spectacle of her former lover in the arms of her best friend was surely more than flesh and blood could endure.

Not that Ken had ever been her lover in any real sense of the word. They had known each other a mere couple of months before Joanne had come along—but Giselle had at one point seriously considered allowing him to be her first. She had waited long enough, she'd decided, for that one special man to come into her life and sweep her off her feet. The warmth, the affection she'd felt for Ken were surely enough to justify such a step.

But it had all been empty daydreams. At a stroke, she'd been reduced to the status of a friend.

Over the painful few months that followed, Ken and Joanne had at least been discreet. Joanne had more or less moved out of the little cottage that she and Giselle officially shared and Ken only rarely showed his face. And the two girls had carried on working together, building up business at Silver Service Catering and trying to pretend that nothing had changed.

But then, just as Giselle was recovering from that first blow, the second bombshell blew up in her face.

This time it was Joanne who broke the news. 'Ken's been offered a job in Marbella—a management job in a big hotel. And it looks as if there might be a job for me too, if I go along with him.'

'But what about us—and Silver Service?'

'I'm sorry, Giselle. I have to opt out.'

And so, with almost indecent haste, their two-year partnership had been dissolved, leaving Giselle virtually penniless in the process and feeling as though her whole world had caved in.

Stop wallowing in self-pity, Davidian had told her. But what could he, with his charmed and pampered lifestyle, possibly know of the misery she'd been through?

She stood up now and, with a shaft of apprehension, glanced down at the order in her hand. A Twenty-four-carat Super Deluxe for a dozen people—and only forty-eight hours in which to prepare it!

But prepare it she would, come hell or high water. She would show him! She had her pride. It didn't matter a damn to her what Fayiz Davidian thought of her, but she would demonstrate, for her own satisfaction, that she was no wallowing, snivelling brat!

The car he had promised arrived at her front door next morning at half-past eight—a vast maroon Mercedes estate big enough to transport a platoon. At the sight of it, Giselle smiled wryly. It was quite an improvement on the old Ford van she'd had to sell when Joanne had walked out!

She could never have managed without it, either. Shortly after nine o'clock, with a shopping list as long as her arm, she was speeding eastwards along the M20 to her favourite fishmonger in Folkestone.

Then back west to Ashford for the truffles and the quails.

By evening she had managed to amass just about all the ingredients she would need—save the seafood and the vegetables that she had arranged to collect first thing the next morning. But, exhausted as she was, there was more work to be done. It was close to midnight when she finally finished the advance preparation of as many of the special stuffings and sauces as could safely be kept in the fridge overnight.

Just after one, she collapsed into bed and slept the dreamless sleep of the virtuous until the alarm woke her at six a.m. sharp.

It was soon after ten when she arrived at Chiltham Hall—by the back entrance this time—and glanced round with admiration and relief at the gargantuan blue-tiled kitchen, equipped with every gismo and gadget that any cook could possibly require. Davidian had been absolutely right: all the equipment she needed was here.

She was dicing vegetables, sleeves rolled to her elbows, when Mrs Pennygreen appeared. 'How are you getting on, my dear?' the woman enquired with a kindly smile. 'That's quite a job you've got on your hands.'

Giselle smiled back bravely in response. 'Oh, don't worry, I'll manage,' she said brightly. 'Everything's under control.'

'I can give you a hand till I finish at five—but don't let on to Mr Davidian!' The housekeeper smiled a conspiratorial smile. 'He gave me strict instructions that I was to leave everything to you.'

Yes, I'll bet he did! Any generous little gesture to make her task as difficult as possible! But, diplomatically, Giselle said nothing, just concentrated on her dicing.

'He worries about my health, you see.' Mrs Pennygreen had pushed up her sleeves and was coming to stand alongside her now. 'I had a bit of a stroke six months ago and the doctors have told me to take things easy.'

Giselle paused in her dicing and turned almost guiltily to look at the woman.

'That's why he refuses to let me do these special dinners any more, and why we get in extra help to do all the heavy jobs.' Mrs Pennygreen frowned. 'But he's too strict, really. Sometimes I feel I'm not earning my pay.'

'Well, I don't believe that for a minute!' Giselle protested. The good woman had loyalty, hard work and diligence stamped all over her kindly face. 'And please don't feel you have to help me,' she added with concern. 'I can manage perfectly on my own.'

That claim had perhaps been slightly over-confident, she was beginning to think around half-past seven. It was that crucial final stage in the preparation of a meal when split-second co-ordination was of the essence and even the most accomplished of cooks felt a twinge of panic. One little hiccup now and the whole carefully constructed gastronomic symphony could fall into discordant disarray. Thank heavens she had at least allowed Mrs Pennygreen to lay the table before signing off!

One thing to be grateful for was that Davidian hadn't shown his face. She had been half expecting—and dreading—that he might suddenly stick his head round the door and start laying down the law. A foolish fear, she now decided, as she put the finishing touches to the stuffed veal. The illustrious Fayiz Davidian probably didn't even know where his kitchen was!

At eight-fifteen, Giselle was hurriedly changing into her navy and white waitress uniform and carefully pinning up her hair beneath the frilly starched white cap. She looked flushed, she decided, hurriedly dabbing on a touch of powder and slicking some lipgloss over her lips. But at least she had made it. The first course was ready and waiting to be served promptly at half-past eight.

She had a rush of nerves when she walked into the dining-room and glanced round at the assembled guests. Fayiz Davidian hadn't been joking when he had told her they were used to the best. The couture clothes and serious-looking jewellery established the truth of that at a glance. But to their eyes she knew she was as good as invisible as she set about her humble task. Only one person in the entire room had even deigned to glance her way, and that person was the powerful, dark-haired man in the immaculate black evening suit who was seated imperiously at the head of the table.

Whatever her personal feelings for him, Giselle had to confess, as she met his glance, that he was looking quite electrifyingly handsome tonight.

The elegant suit, black bow tie and the vivid whiteness of his shirt both emphasised and simultaneously softened his faintly harsh, exotic good looks. Even the glamorous, dark-haired girl at his side paled into mediocrity by comparison. And from the effortless poise with which he presided over the gathering, Giselle could tell that the panther was in total command!

To her own incalculable relief, she also managed to remain in command of her side of the operation. Apart from a near disaster with the chocolate sauce for the profiteroles, the meal went off without a hitch. And, judging by the satisfyingly empty plates that were stacked up by the kitchen sink, her efforts had also been enjoyed. Her marathon finally over, she slumped down gratefully on a kitchen stool and poured herself a glass of wine.

'Congratulations. That was a first-class job.'

At the unexpected sound of the deep, velvet voice, Giselle spun round, startled, and laid down her drink. Fayiz Davidian was standing in the doorway, half smiling, watching her.

She pushed back a stray strand of hair from her face—so he did, after all, know his way to the kitchen!—and answered him, slightly resenting this intrusion. For the first time in two gruelling days she had been about to relax! 'I'm glad it came up to your exacting standards,' she retorted with an edge of sarcasm in her voice.

'It more than came up to them. It surpassed them.' He walked towards her across the tiled floor, hands in the pockets of his trousers, and came to a halt just a few feet away. 'As I said, you did a magnificent job. My clients and their wives were most impressed.'

He looked so devilishly handsome, so immaculately poised that Giselle was all at once uncomfortably conscious of her own comparatively limp and bedraggled state. She straightened her shoulders defensively and smoothed the rumpled skirt of her dress, as she slid down slowly from the stool and deliberately averted her eyes from his face. 'That's nice to know,' she answered tightly, as she began to gather dirty glasses on to a tray. 'I imagine such people are not easily impressed.'

'Indeed they are not. Particularly the wives. The peacocks' feathers, as I like to call them.'

Giselle turned to look at him. 'Peacocks' feathers?' What on earth did he mean by that?

With a faint smile, he reached out and lifted up one of the long-stemmed Baccarat wine glasses. Momentarily, it caught the light and flashed. 'Like peacocks' feathers, they serve no useful function, except for show and decoration, to reflect the wealth and status of their men. From time to time, as an indulgence, I allow them to grace my table.'

So he had started already with his chauvinist comments! Giselle's eyes narrowed with dislike. 'Yet I couldn't help noticing,' she observed cuttingly, referring to his dark-haired dinner companion, 'that you're not above donning a few feathers yourself.'

He shook his head and fixed her with those eyes. 'The peacock's feathers are secured firmly in its tail—in human terms, they are fiancées and wives. The lady you refer to, I'm afraid, occupies no such secure position in my life.' He laid the glass down on the tray. 'A mere bauble, for dinner parties and the like.'

Deliberately, Giselle looked away. The man was insufferable, and she had no desire to listen to another single one of his anti-female gibes. In a tight voice she told him, 'Well, it was very thoughtful of you indeed to make this little detour to express your appreciation of the meal.' She gathered up more dirty glasses. Perhaps now he would go.

He did not go. Instead he said, 'Actually, that wasn't all I came for. I came to invite you through for a drink.'

'A drink?' She glanced up, blinking, from the tray of glasses, as though unfamiliar with this word.

'My guests have gone and, after all your hard work, I thought you might like to relax over a brandy.'

How very civilised! It sounded tempting. Yet somehow Giselle could not quite envisage herself sharing a cosy decanter of brandy with the illustrious Fayiz Davidian. Abruptly she turned her attention back to the glasses. 'I'm afraid I haven't finished clearing up. There are all these dirty dishes to see to yet.'

Out of the corner of her eye she saw him shrug. 'The dishwasher will take care of these. There's no need for you to waste time washing up.' So, not only did he know where to find the kitchen, he knew it boasted a dishwasher too! Then he proceeded to astound her further as he stepped towards her now and offered, 'I'll give you a hand to load it, then we can go through and have that drink.'

There was something jarringly incongruous about the picture presented by the tall, dark-suited man stacking piles of dirty porcelain into the machine. Yet his demeanour was so totally devoid of self-consciousness that one might almost have supposed that he regularly performed such menial tasks. Giselle found herself watching him with suspicion. The more she observed of Fayiz Davidian, the more of a mystery he became.

The task accomplished, he proceeded to lead her from the kitchen down a long, wide corridor to the front of the house. Giselle had discarded her apron and the starched white frilly cap, surreptitiously unpinning her hair so that it fell to her shoulders in a corona of soft curls. But she still felt faintly ill at ease as she followed his broad, dark, swiftly moving back through an imposing doorway into a large reception room.

What had prompted this unlikely invitation? What did Davidian have on his mind?

'Make yourself comfortable. Take a seat.' He was waving her towards a cluster of soft leather sofas of the type one sees featured in the more expensive glossy magazines. Just a touch awkwardly, Giselle obliged, poising herself on the edge of one of the deeply cushioned seats as he crossed to a table in one corner where some bottles and glasses were laid out.

As he turned with his back to her, she glanced quickly round. The room was quite inordinately beautiful, yet surprisingly welcoming and informal. The clever work, no doubt, of some high-flying professional decorator, it bore none of those hard-edged, faintly forbidding qualities that characterised its owner. On the contrary, it radiated warmth, bathed as it was in the peachy glow cast by two huge silk-shaded table lamps.

'Cognac?' her host was asking, holding aloft a bottle of Courvoisier VSOP. 'Or would you prefer something else?'

'Cognac's fine. But just a very small one, please.' For one thing, she had no desire to linger; for another, she had even less desire to get even the slightest bit tipsy in his presence. And in her current state of extreme fatigue it would take but a thimbleful of the Courvoisier to start blurring her senses and slowing her reflexes—a highly inadvisable state to be in when dealing with a man like Fayiz Davidian!

'So . . . How does it feel?' he enquired enigmatically, coming across the room towards her, a brandy glass in either hand.

As he paused in front of her and handed her one, Giselle observed with some surprise that he had in fact poured her a tiny measure. Most people, she knew, out of misguided generosity, would simply have ignored her request. With a sense of unease—what made this man tick?—she looked up into the fathomless black eyes. 'How does *what* feel?' she wanted to know.

He seated himself in the sofa opposite and took a mouthful of his drink. 'How does it feel,' he elaborated slowly, 'to have achieved the impossible?' As she frowned, he reached out to deposit the brandy glass on a small glass-topped table to one side and scanned her face with a penetrating look. 'Two days ago you told me that for you to prepare tonight's dinner alone was an outright impossibility.' He paused for a moment, eyes fixed on her face. 'And yet you did it—quite admirably, I may say. You must be feeling extremely proud of yourself.'

'I feel exhausted, if you want to know the truth. It's something I would never attempt again.'

'But proud of yourself, none the less,' he insisted.

Giselle knew exactly what he was getting at, but she was reluctant to go along the path where he was leading her. She shrugged. 'I'm just relieved it's over, and that I survived to tell the tale.' Though, in fact, he was right, she did feel proud. And more than just proud. Immensely reassured. Her morale of late had taken such a terrible beating that to have succeeded in meeting this considerable challenge with such a wholehearted degree of success had restored some of her flagging faith in herself.

'Do you still wish that I'd allowed you to pass on the contract to some other caterers?'

She met his eyes levelly, resenting this line of questioning. 'It would have made life considerably easier for me.' Did he perhaps expect her to thank him, to admit that, perversely, he'd done her a favour? He was in for a disappointment if he did. But, characteristically, he threw her with his next remark.

'And is that what you want? An easy life?'

There was an edge of scorn to the mild reproof, that familiar edge of scorn she had sensed before. For some reason she felt herself colour guiltily as she shifted self-consciously in her seat. 'Doesn't everyone?' she countered.

Fayiz Davidian narrowed his eyes and ran long, strong fingers down the side of his jaw. After a pause that seemed to last for a lifetime, he responded at last, dismissively, 'The wishes and desires of others are not something I can answer for. And, speaking as one who has no personal experience of the merits or otherwise of an easy life, I find myself uniquely unqualified to pass judgement on its desirability.'

In spite of the dark look in his eyes, Giselle could not quite suppress a guffaw. Did he honestly expect her to believe that, sitting here surrounded by all this luxury? 'Forgive me,' she told him, tossing back her hair, 'but to an outsider like me that is scarcely how it seems.'

He allowed himself a shadow of a smile. 'No doubt,' he agreed. 'But then outsiders are rarely in a position to see the entire picture, as I'm sure you would agree?' The dark eyes held hers for a moment and, with a flicker of curiosity, Giselle found herself waiting. Was he about to reveal some deep, dark personal secret to her?

Indeed he was not. Instead, with easy adroitness, he turned the conversation around. 'So tell me, Miss Copeland,' he enquired with more than a hint of mockery in his tone, 'how do you plan on achieving this easy life you tell me you're after?'

Giselle toyed impatiently with the brandy glass in her hand and felt sorely tempted just to get up and go. He had this infernal ability to paint her into a corner and put into her mouth words she had never meant to say. But he also had the complementary effect of making her feel anxious to defend herself. So she stayed where she was and told him tersely, 'I intend to work for it, that's how.'

'Ah, I see.' The dark head nodded in what might have passed for approval had not she caught the flicker of cynicism in his eyes. He reached for his brandy glass and took a mouthful. 'I take it that means that you intend to resurrect Silver Service Catering?'

If only that were possible, Giselle thought to herself as with a stab of gloom she glanced down into her lap. In spite of the hectic pressures of the past couple of days, nothing would have pleased her better. But how could she even think of such a thing when, after all, nothing had changed? The proceeds from tonight, though most welcome, were scarcely enough to put her back in business.

Despondently she shook her head. 'No, I'm afraid I'll have to get a job.'

'What sort of a job?'

'In some hotel or restaurant, I suppose.' She was, after all, a qualified cook.

Fayiz Davidian shook his head. 'That sounds to me a most unlikely route to the easy life,' he observed.

Giselle's eyes flicked up, resenting his sarcasm. It was easy for him to be so damned superior! 'It does to me too,' she told him coldly, 'but I'm afraid I have no choice. I have a bank loan I have to pay back, so I need a steady job. And, since catering is the only work I'm qualified for, there aren't very many options open to me.'

The dark eyes swept her from top to toe. 'You surprise me,' he said with a lift of one eyebrow.

She looked back at him. 'Surprise you—how?'

'I would have thought a girl like you . . .' he let his voice trail off before adding '. . . would have several options open to her.'

And what exactly did he mean by that? Giselle straightened angrily in her seat, suddenly disturbingly aware of how the dark eyes were lazily scanning her form, moving like a sensuous, slow caress over the ample swell of her breasts beneath the constricting dark navy uniform, curving appreciatively round her hips and thighs, then sweeping the shapely length of her calves to pause for a moment at her ankles. 'What options did you have in mind?' she demanded hotly.

Without answering, Davidian loosened his tie,

his eyes drifting upwards to her face, and she thought she saw the hint of a smile curve suggestively round the wide, carved lips. He leaned back a little in his seat and surveyed her unhurriedly through lowered lids, at the same time leisurely crossing his legs so that one ankle rested on the opposite knee. Long, copper-skinned fingers curled around the ankle, somehow inevitably drawing her eyes to the hard, sinuous lines of his calves and thighs outlined beneath the fabric of his trousers.

And all at once she was almost painfully conscious of a startling reality that had so far escaped her. Here she was, sitting alone in this vast, empty house, in the notoriously dangerous wee small hours, with possibly the most sexually unsettling man she had ever encountered in her life. Nervously, she gulped back the brandy in her glass and averted her eyes as at last he said, 'I can think of several options, but one in particular springs to mind.'

'Oh, yes. And what might that be?' She had to ask the question, though she was far from certain she wanted to know the answer. She had the strangest, most uncomfortable feeling that he was about to make some wild and improper proposition.

Long fingers caressed the silk-clad ankle, moving briefly to touch the bench-made shoe. He had this unselfconscious animal sensuality that seemed to filter into every move he made. Panther-like, Giselle found herself thinking again, as, in that low, faintly ominous panther-like purr, he enquired, 'Would you consider moving to London?'

'London?' She looked across at him without comprehension, almost as though he'd said Timbuctoo.

The panther smiled. 'Belgravia, to be precise.'

'Belgravia?' Again, stupidly, she found herself repeating what he had just said. The truth was, she was inwardly squirming, wondering exactly what he had up his sleeve.

He leaned towards her with a flicker of impatience. 'Well, would you?' he wanted to know.

Giselle took a mouthful from her empty glass, then, feeling foolish, dropped it to her lap. 'What's in Belgravia that could possibly interest me?'

The dark eyes held hers for a moment. 'Me,' he answered in a word.

'You?'

'Me. That's where I live when I'm not here.'

How very nice for you, she thought to herself. Aloud she answered, 'So? I don't understand.'

Fayiz Davidian uncrossed his legs, then spread them wide as he leaned towards her, hands clasped loosely, elbows on thighs, and told her in a matter-of-fact tone, 'I have a very large apartment just off Eaton Square. Plenty of rooms, plenty of space. Certainly more than enough for two.'

He paused.

Giselle swallowed.

Then he half smiled as he continued, 'I do a lot of entertaining there, especially during the summer months. I need someone. A young woman like yourself . . .' He paused again, the dark eyes unblinking, as she stared back at him, dry-mouthed. Then he put to her what was on his mind, as though he made such offers every day of his life . . .

'The question I'm asking is really very simple . . . Would you consider leaving here and moving into my London flat with me?'

CHAPTER THREE

IT WAS perfectly evident, Giselle was thinking, as she sat there, tongue-tied, staring at him in horror, that the man had taken temporary leave of his senses.

Stiff-fingered, she laid aside her empty brandy glass and drew herself up on the leather sofa. 'I don't think I understand what you mean, Mr Davidian,' she answered cautiously in a cool, distant tone—though, privately, she was thinking that she understood only too well. All at once, it was quite outrageously clear what had been behind his unexpected invitation to join him for a drink. And this sleazy proposition he had just made was really not worthy of either of them.

Fayiz Davidian met her eyes, unabashedly unrepentant. 'What is there not to understand?' he enquired. 'I'm offering you a job, Miss Copeland.'

Giselle blinked. Then she blinked again. Could it be she had misunderstood? 'A job?' she repeated, still half disbelieving. 'Exactly what kind of job?'

'Exactly the kind of job you're qualified to do. A job as my private resident caterer.' As she continued to blink at him, he went on to explain, 'As you may already be aware, I run an investment company in the City—which is to say it's my job to advise my clients on how best to invest their money . . .'

As he paused, she nodded in the affirmative.

44

'Yes, I was aware that you did something like that.'

He leaned back a little in his seat and ran the palm of one hand across his dark hair. 'A lot of my clients are from the Middle East. Since I come from that part of the world myself, I speak their language, in every sense.' He dropped his hand on to the arm of the sofa, the long bronzed fingers spreading out to idly caress the butter-soft leather. 'Since they tend to choose this time of year—namely, summer—to visit London, it also tends to be the time of year when I'm at my busiest. I like to keep things as personal as possible,' he told her, his eyes still fixed on her face, 'so I arrange private little dinner parties at my flat where I can discuss business with my clients in an informal atmosphere.'

He paused and threw her a provocative smile. 'And that, Miss Copeland, is where you come in.'

'You mean you want to hire me to come to London to prepare your dinner parties for you?'

He nodded. 'That's precisely what I want.'

She was tempted to ask: Why me? He could, after all, afford to hire anyone he wanted. Instead, evasively, she told him, 'I'm not really sure I'd be suitable for the job.'

'Why ever not?' He sounded surprised. 'As you've just proved tonight, you're an excellent cook—and your table service is both accomplished and discreet. You're exactly what I'm looking for.' He went on to explain, 'In the past I've always hired outside caterers and the service they have provided has been beyond reproach—but I have had the occasional problem when I've needed something at very short notice. Hence my decision to hire a caterer of my own.'

As she continued to watch him with doubt in her eyes, he added reassuringly, 'If you're worried that you might be expected to provide regular dinners for a dozen people, let me put your mind at rest. My dinner parties in Belgravia tend to be very small, very private affairs. I rarely entertain more than two or three clients at once.'

But that particular reservation was not what was uppermost in Giselle's mind. Her overriding concern was much simpler and more fundamental. For how could she seriously consider an arrangement that involved not only working for, but also living within the same four walls as Fayiz Davidian? The very prospect made her shudder. However big his apartment might be, it could never be big enough to make such an arrangement endurable. In fact, she strongly suspected, there was nothing in the world that could possibly do that!

Well, almost nothing . . .

'Naturally, I would pay you well. Considerably above the going rate.' He named a figure that made her jaw drop. 'I think that, financially, you would find it worthwhile.'

Worthwhile was putting it mildly. He had just named a sum for three months' work that it would normally have taken her at least twice as long to earn! But if she was thinking he was offering her easy money, he was eager to disabuse her of that notion straight away.

'In exchange, I would expect you to be on call every day and to work whatever hours are necessary. If I need you seven days a week, twenty-four hours a day, that's exactly what I'll expect you to do. Sometimes you may be required to whip up a meal at very short notice, so either myself or one of my staff must always know where you are and how to reach you.' He paused and fixed her with a steely glance. 'Have no fear, you will earn every penny.'

But Giselle had never found hard work daunting. She looked back at him levelly and answered, 'On that score, Mr Davidian, you need have no fear either.'

'So?' He smiled that fleeting, shadowy smile that occasionally lightened his harsh, dark features and looked across at her curiously now. 'Are you tempted by my offer, Miss Copeland?' he queried.

Sorely, sorely tempted, she admitted reluctantly to herself. Already her mind was racing as she calculated breathlessly how much she could save. A considerable sum, she realised, since she would have neither her board nor overheads to pay for. And if she could sublet the cottage for the summer, then she would be even better off.

Her brain cells were buzzing like a switched-on computer as she rolled the figures around in her head. At the end of it all, with a bit of luck, she could well be left with more than enough to buy a new van, replace the various bits of equipment she'd sold and resurrect Silver Service Catering—with herself in sole and glorious charge.

It was a dream come true. A gift from the gods.

But there had to be a catch, of course. Nothing was for nothing, as she well knew. And the catch was sitting right there opposite her, watching her with demonic black eyes. A gift from the gods indeed! Would it not rather be sheer, unbridled folly even to think of entering into such an agreement with a man like Fayiz Davidian?

As he waited for her answer, a thought occurred to her. 'In view of your low opinion of women, I'm slightly surprised that you would propose such an arrangement. You told me women are unreliable, not to be trusted professionally.'

He raised one dark eyebrow. 'Do you support that theory?'

'Of course not! I was merely repeating what you said.'

He shook his head slowly and regarded her clinically as he proceeded to correct her now. 'What I said, Miss Copeland, was that it was an unwise man—or woman, for that matter—who would enter into a partnership with a woman. But, since nothing could be further from my mind, I fail to see what relevance that has now.'

As he paused, regarding her from beneath sooty black lashes, Giselle said nothing, just glared at him in silence. Trust him to remember, verbatim, what he had told her at their first meeting!

He smiled at her with all the warmth of a cobra, as he continued to put her right. 'Let's be absolutely clear from the start, the arrangement I have in mind is in no way some kind of partnership, Miss

Copeland. I employ you and I'm the boss. I tell you what to do and you do it—and I can fire you whenever I wish.' Another pause. Another cold smile. 'Which, should you fail to live up to our contract—to be unreliable, in other words—I assure you I shall do without a second thought.'

Giselle did not doubt it for a minute. Nor did she doubt that, as an employer and boss, Fayiz Davidian would crack a mean whip. The other day she had caught a glimpse of how hard he drove himself, working even on a Sunday and, most probably, Saturdays and Bank Holidays too. He would think nothing of demanding the same of her. And on top of that there would be the added pressure of having to share an apartment with him. She gave a little inward shiver. She could cope with all the hard work he could throw at her, but she was far from certain she could cope with him!

'So, Miss Copeland?' He was watching her. 'How does my proposition sound?'

Giselle wavered and did not answer. Frankly, she could have told him, his proposition sounded like hell. Three long miserable months of sheer, unmitigated hell. A life sentence on Devil's Island, by comparison, would have sounded like a holiday. She opened her mouth to express the sentiment. 'I'm sorry, Mr Davidian, I really don't think . . .' But then, abruptly, her voice trailed off as she thought of the large sum of money involved. How could she turn her back on that when, with it, she could save Silver Service Catering?

'You don't think what, Miss Copeland?' He

was waiting.

'I don't think . . .' She floundered helplessly, resenting the cleft stick he'd caught her in. 'I don't think . . .' she began again, her mind still reeling this way and that. Then she straightened in her seat and took the coward's way out—procrastination. 'I can't possibly make a decision without first giving the matter a little thought.'

'What is there to think about? You need a job and I'm offering you one.'

'Someone else may offer me a better one.' He was so damned arrogant, but she would not be bulldozed!

He laughed softly, dismissively, as he leaned back in his seat, touching the tips of his long fingers together and resting them lightly against his chin. 'Like what?' he demanded, then went on to answer the question himself. 'Like some two-bit position in the steamy kitchen of some hotel, working long, unsocial hours for a pittance at the end of it? Or in some little country coffee-shop, making pancakes and scones for an equal pittance?'

He laughed again, in that scornful manner, and shook his glossy dark head at her. 'Continue to think small, Miss Copeland, and you can forget about ever running your own business again. But then I reckon you don't deserve to. As you said yourself, you want things easy. You're not prepared to make sacrifices or take risks. No doubt you would prefer some man to take them for you, then hand you the proceeds on a plate.' His lip curled. His voice was a snarl. 'Well, congratulations, Miss Copeland. It's the oldest female trick in the book.'

It was as though he'd thrown vitriol in her face. Momentarily, Giselle felt stunned. Not a single word of that vicious diatribe in any way represented the truth. He had deliberately twisted and distorted everything she'd ever said. On a wave of outrage, she sprang to her feet and glared down at him with contempt in her eyes.

'You're wrong, Mr Davidian!' she declared with feeling. 'None of the reasons you've just cited have anything to do with why I don't want your job! If you really want to know the truth, the simple fact of the matter is that I couldn't stomach working for you! You're the most chauvinistic, overbearing man I've ever had the misfortune to meet. Believe me, I'd much sooner work in some steamy hotel kitchen for the pittance you mentioned than have to put up with a rude bully like you!'

She had expected her outburst to provoke a show of anger, but his tone was calm, though steely, as he observed, 'As I said, Miss Copeland, you're not prepared to make the necessary sacrifices. You want it all handed to you on a plate.'

As she stood there, poised and ready to flounce out of the room, Davidian rose slowly to his feet, stepping in front of her, blocking her path. '*I am* prepared to make the sacrifices,' he continued, fixing her with those piercing ebony eyes, 'and that's the difference between us, you see. For I hope you're not labouring under the misconception that it would be anything less than a burden to me to have a continuously whining young female like yourself kicking around my feet all summer. It would not be hard to find someone equally able—and infinitely more agreeable.'

'Then do so!'

'Is that your final word?'

It was on the tip of her tongue to blurt out 'Yes!' and have done once and for all with the whole wretched business. Just then, beneath the barrage of his insults, the money he was offering had suddenly seemed paltry in comparison with the abuse she would have to suffer. But what held her back was the sudden knowledge that, by turning down his offer, she might, unintentionally, be doing him a favour. Hadn't he just more or less said that he would find her presence disagreeable? That thought somehow added to the appeal of his offer.

'Well?' He was standing over her, a darkly vibrant male presence, faintly unsettling in his warm proximity. 'I'm afraid I need your answer now. I'm returning to London early tomorrow morning.' As she hesitated, he started to turn away, his tone contemptuous as he told her, 'No, I didn't think you had it in you to accept such a challenge. In fact, if I were a betting man, I would have laid heavy odds against it.'

He would, would he? 'Then you would have lost.' All at once, of its own volition, her hand reached out to take hold of his arm. She sought his eyes with a provocative smile. 'I'm accepting your offer, Mr Davidian,' she said.

He paused then and turned towards her, the dark eyes gliding downwards to the hand that, unconsciously, still lingered on his sleeve. 'I see.'

He smiled insinuatingly as she continued to look him squarely in the eye. 'My offer, however, was confined to catering. Let us be absolutely clear about that. If it is your intention to seek to make your life a little easier by getting round me with your womanly wiles, I'm afraid I'd better warn you right now that such tactics are a waste of time.'

Somehow he'd misunderstood entirely! She'd intended to irritate, not to appease. 'But I—— You——!' Incoherently, she started to protest. But as she snatched her hand away, he caught it in his, his touch burningly, searingly, warm to her flesh.

Then, with his free hand, he lightly captured her jaw, twisting her face round to look up into his. 'However, should you wish to get friendly, simply for the hell of it, I'd be only too willing to oblige. But not tonight, I'm afraid, Miss Copeland. It's been a long and rather tiring day.'

Giselle's brain was frothing with indignation. 'I've never been more insulted in all my life!' As he continued, mockingly, to hold her captive, she struggled to snatch herself free from his grip, breasts heaving beneath her navy uniform, her heart hammering wildly against her ribs.

'What's the matter, didn't you think I'd take you up on your generous offer? Did you think you'd get away with a harmless little tease?'

Tease? The man had taken leave of his senses! Nothing had been further from her mind! But somehow, though she opened her mouth to speak, she couldn't find the words to tell him so. His nearness, his warmth, his powerful vibrancy, so totally overwhelmingly and threateningly male, seemed all at once to have robbed her of the power of coherent speech. She gulped air helplessly, like a fish in a net. 'Let me go!' was all she could manage to protest, her voice a faint and throaty croak.

The dark eyes pierced her like burning daggers. 'Surely not, *habibiti*,' he murmured, 'without giving you a taste of the riches to come?'

Then, almost before she realised what he intended, he was pulling her to him, roughly, his arms closing about her like bands of steel. As her lips parted soundlessly to protest, her breasts were crushed against the hard wall of his chest and she caught just a glint of burning black eyes as his lips came down to conquer hers.

And, through her outrage, her blood was pounding, her senses hopelessly, deliciously inflamed by the sensuous mastery of that ravishing kiss.

His fingers were in her hair, dragging against her scalp, sending scalding hot flickers of excitement dancing up and down her spine. His other hand was curved around her waist, in a downward caressing path, then, abruptly, he clasped her firm female buttocks to urge her hips into contact with his. The intimacy of the movement made her catch her breath as she felt his desire press hard against her belly. Yet, along with the shaft of shock that shot through her, a fire ignited shamelessly in her loins.

Then his hand was sweeping up between their bodies, sure and firm, to cup her breast, circling, caressing, tearing at her senses, making her groan deep in her throat. Never in her life before had her body responded like this to a man.

'OK, *habibiti*, that will do for now.' To her shame and confusion, all at once he released her and looked down at her with scornful, detached eyes. 'We can take it from there some other time. That was just by way of an appetiser.'

'You . . .! You . . .!' Giselle was tugging at the front of her dress—two buttons had come undone, she was mortified to see—jabbing her fingers through her rumpled hair, trembling with anger and shame and outrage. 'How dare you?' she accused, her gold eyes flashing. 'How dare you take such liberties with me?'

He arched one coal-black eyebrow at her, quite unmoved by her remonstrations. 'That was just to let you see, my dear Miss Copeland, that she who plays with me plays with fire.' He paused, then spelled out his lesson further. 'And she who plays with fire gets burnt.' With one last crushing glance at her, he turned away towards the door. 'And now, if you don't mind, I'll drive you home. Tomorrow I have a very early start.'

Giselle was suddenly speechless through her fury. Blindly she followed his broad back to the door, hating him within an inch of his life. Fayiz Davidian, she was fast concluding, was the most arrogant, detestable man on this earth!

But he was wrong if he thought he could control her, or that she had any intention of getting burnt. From now on, she'd be learning her lesson—and fighting fire with fire!

He gave her three days to get organised and move up to London. 'I shall expect to see you at the flat on Friday,' he told her in that autocratic tone of his, as he dropped her off home at two in the morning. 'I have a pretty full weekend of entertaining arranged.'

It was a blessing in disguise, Giselle decided, that he should demand her presence in such a hurry. That way she had little time to dwell upon the gravity of her decision. Three months working for, and living with, Fayiz Davidian promised to be a taste of hell on earth!

Still, what choice did she have, looking at the situation through realistic eyes? There was no other way, within so short a period, that she could earn the sort of money he was offering. And that money was her future and her independence - the latter of vital importance to her, in spite of Davidian's scathing suggestions to the contrary.

What type of women must he have encountered in his life, she found herself wondering more and more, to have developed such a total and all-consuming contempt for the female of the species?

By a stroke of immense good fortune, she managed to sublet her cottage for the summer. The niece of an old client from the village was looking for somewhere quiet for a few months to write up her university thesis - and what could possibly be more quiet than Honeybee Cottage, near Old

Wives Lees, right in the heart of rural Kent?

Giselle felt like hugging herself. Now, for the next three months, she would have virtually no expenses at all. She would be able to save almost every penny that Davidian was paying her. And save she would! she vowed to herself. She would not allow herself to be seduced by the glittering shop windows of London. Not that she would likely have much time for such self-indulgence, anyway. If Davidian was true to his threat—and somehow she had no doubt that he would be—after work, she would have very little time or energy to spare for anything except sleeping!

Just after four o'clock on Friday afternoon, after travelling up from Kent by rail, she took the London Underground to Sloane Square station, in the heart of ultra-smart Belgravia. Then, armed with her two small battered cases, she made her way on foot to the address Davidian had given her, just off Eaton Square.

So this was where the other half lived! She glanced round with curiosity at the Rolls-Royces and Bentleys parked along the pavement's edge, at the elegant, imposing buildings with their uniformed doormen in attendance, catching occasional, tantalising glimpses of the incredible luxury that lay beyond.

If the streets of London were paved with gold, as the stories of her childhood had told, those currently beneath her feet were the genuine twenty-four-carat variety! The unmistakable scent of money hung like rose blossom in the air.

Needless to mention, the building that housed Davidian's apartment was the most sumptuous of all.

Feeling like a refugee, with one battered old suitcase in either hand, she waited by the desk in the vast, mirrored entrance hall while the doorman rang upstairs to check the credentials of this unlikely-looking visitor.

'Right you are, miss. You're expected.' He smiled and led her towards the lift. 'Just press "P", the very top button. Mr Davidian's is the penthouse flat.'

Well, it would be wouldn't it? Giselle thought resentfully to herself, as the elevator whisked her in sumptuous silence up to the very top of the building. Hadn't she decided long ago that Davidian was one of those blessed individuals upon whom fate could not pour enough of her riches? Yet he had had the audacity to accuse her of looking for an easy life!

A tiny Filipino maid, as pretty as a picture, was waiting by the open door. 'Miss Copeland?' she enquired with a smile. Then, as Giselle nodded, she invited, 'Please come in. Mr Davidian isn't back from the office yet, so I'll show you to your room.'

Giselle followed the dainty figure across a marble-tiled entrance hall and down a wide corridor illuminated by chandeliers. Had she been alone, she would have paused for a closer look at her surroundings. Did people really live like this? she was asking herself in bemused disbelief. The elaborately moulded and corniced ceilings were high enough to accommodate a jumbo jet, the paintings on the walls rivalled those of the Louvre and there appeared to be enough rooms in the place to house an entire battalion of the Grenadier Guards!

A door at the end of the corridor was pushed open and Giselle followed the maid into the room beyond. 'This will be your room,' the girl informed her. 'It has its own en-suite bathroom, of course.'

Of course. Giselle nodded. 'It's very nice.' Which was really the very least she could say. The most luxurious bedroom she'd ever occupied before had been in a four-star hotel while on holiday in Greece. But that had been a broom cupboard compared to this! She glanced round appreciatively at the silk-clad bed, in a delicate shade of blue to match the extravagantly swagged curtains, at the gilded furnishings and watered silk walls, then turned once more to look at the maid. 'Quite a house Mr Davidian has here!'

The girl smiled. 'Quite a house. Very different,' she agreed.

'Very different?' Giselle laughed, appreciating the understatement. 'It's certainly very different from anything I've ever known!'

But apparently she had misunderstood. The dark-haired girl shook her head. 'I mean it's very different now from what it was like before.'

'You mean it's recently been redecorated?'

The girl nodded. 'After Mrs Davidian left last year, Mr Davidian had the whole place changed.' She clucked a faintly disapproving tongue. 'And it had only been done just a year before.' As Giselle frowned down at her, she glanced away and abruptly began to back out the door, swiftly changing the subject, as though fearing she might already have said too much.

'I'll leave you to get settled in—just make yourself at home once you've unpacked.—and I'll see you again tomorrow morning.' She paused and smiled. 'My name's Ella, by the way. I'm here between seven and four o'clock, normally. I like to get home before my husband, Eddie, finishes his shift at the hospital.' Her smile broadened proudly. 'He's a nurse.'

'Oh. That's nice,' Giselle nodded automatically, then, politely, she apologised, 'I'm sorry if I kept you late. I'm afraid the trains rather let me down.'

'No problem,' Ella assured her. 'I was happy to wait for you.' Then she added quickly before she closed the door, 'Mr Davidian said to tell you that he'd be home just after six.'

Left alone, Giselle sank down on the bed and stared for a long moment into space. She felt faintly shell-shocked, though she couldn't think why. What possible difference in the world did the girl's revelation make to her?

For amid all the routine bits and pieces that the Filipino maid had told her—about the house, her husband and her working hours—there was one outstanding piece of information that had taken Giselle quite unawares. And which was buzzing around inside her brain now, as bothersome as a bluebottle trapped against a window-pane.

The mysterious Fayiz Davidian, it appeared, was not the footloose bachelor she had supposed. According to Ella, there was a *Mrs* Davidian. Fayiz Davidian had a wife!

CHAPTER FOUR

SO now was added a new dimension to the enigma that was Fayiz Davidian.

Giselle unpacked her two small suitcases and hung their contents in the vast fitted wardrobes, her movements automatic, unthinking, her mind still fixed on the maid's revelation. And, through the shock and surprise she felt, she was aware of a growing sense of anger. Fayiz Davidian's marital status might be fundamentally none of her business, but surely, in the circumstances, it would have been more proper if he had told her. It suddenly began to seem not quite right that she should be living here when he had a wife.

A wife who had walked out on him, by all accounts, she pondered curiously, recalling Ella's words. And whose departure had prompted him to lavish thousands of extravagant pounds totally refurbishing their flat. In order, presumably, to obliterate all trace of her.

Giselle smiled a bitter smile to herself. The intensity and suppressed violence implicit in that gesture seemed in total keeping with the character of the man. She felt a sudden stab of sympathy and sistership for Davidian's estranged spouse. It was not too difficult to appreciate what must have driven her away.

Three hours later, just after eight, she was feeling

even more sympathy for Mrs Davidian. He had told Ella to tell her he would be home around six, yet he still hadn't shown up, or even phoned. No doubt his poor long-suffering wife had had to put up with this sort of treatment all the time. Like everything else, Giselle suspected, she would have been required to take second place to his work.

In the meantime, Giselle had helped herself to some chicken salad she'd found in the fridge and had treated herself to a discreet tour of the flat. And on closer inspection, she found, it was even more breathtaking than at first glance—in spite of the fact that, here and there, the faultless décor betrayed the uncompromisingly masculine hand of its owner. The deep clarets of the drawing-room furnishings, the heavy-framed pictures that adorned the walls, the traditional antique furniture.

Yet there was a surprising air of informality about it all, just as she had noticed at Chiltham Hall—a quality she might have described as 'homely' were not such an epithet hopelessly inappropriate when used in association with Fayiz Davidian!

She stepped out through the drawing-room balcony windows and gazed out over the lights of Belgravia towards magnificent Green Park with, off to the west, a glimpse of Hyde Park and the gently flowing Serpentine. Then she leaned against the balcony railings, shaking back her Titian hair, and breathed in deeply, closing her eyes.

She would make the most of this taste of the good life, she resolved, and enjoy every moment to the hilt. In spite of the hard graft that lay ahead of her.

And, most important of all, in spite of Davidian.

'Good evening, Miss Copeland. Enjoying the view?'

She swung round, startled, catching her breath, to find him watching her from the balcony doorway. He was dressed in a pearl-grey suit, with an eye-catching silver-grey tie and the habitual immaculate white shirt. His hands were casually in the pockets of his trousers as he crossed the balcony towards her. She cleared her throat. 'Good evening, Mr Davidian.'

He paused just a metre or so away. 'I hope I didn't startle you?'

'You did a little.' Her heart was still pounding quite ludicrously and warm colour had risen to her cheeks. She turned away with her back towards him and looked out over the city again. 'As you say, I was admiring the view. It's very beautiful at this time of night.'

'You're right, it is. It's my favourite time. When the lights come on and all the commuters have gone home, that's when London is at its most civilised.' He had come alongside her to share the view. She could glimpse, from the corner of her eye, the strong bronzed hands on the balcony rail. Then, glancing round at her, he said, 'I trust you weren't too bored while you were waiting and that you've helped yourself to something to eat? I'm afraid, as usual, I got held up.'

'Yes, I've eaten.' Her tone was clipped. She was, for some reason, deeply irritated by this offhand apology for his lateness. An excuse for an apology, that was all it was. Though she suspected it was probably the closest to a proper apology that a man like Fayiz Davidian ever got.

He seemed not to notice, or not to care. He straightened. 'I suggest we go indoors. I have a pile of papers to get through before I turn in tonight and I ought to explain to you about the dinner tomorrow evening.' Without bothering to wait for her response, he turned and led the way indoors. With fierce irritation, she glared at his back. She was evidently just expected to follow.

He sat in one of the deep claret armchairs and invited her to take another nearby. Then, from the table at his elbow, he took a crystal decanter and poured into one of the matching glasses a modest measure of what looked like brandy. He glanced across at her, holding up the glass. 'Would you care to join me in a cognac?' he asked.

In the light of the drawing-room she could see the dark shadows that cast pools of tiredness around his eyes. But she felt no sympathy, only a deepening irritation. If he drove himself so relentlessly it was because he wished to. Surely there was nothing in the world to prevent a man of Davidian's position and wealth working normal office hours? She declined his offer of a drink. 'No, thanks, I won't, if you don't mind.'

Fortunately, he made no effort to press her. It was clearly of not the slightest consequence to him whether she chose to join him or not. He leaned back and took a long, slow mouthful, resting his head against the back of the chair, his hair black and glossy as polished jet against the rich red silk damask. He laid his hand, still holding the glass, along the deeply curved arm of the chair and observed, glancing down at it, as though talking to himself, 'It'll be straight in at the deep end tomorrow evening. I'm entertaining Sheikh Hamad.' The dark eyes flicked up. He threw her a smile. 'Sheikh Hamad and his brother, Sheikh Abdulaziz.'

All at once Giselle was wishing that she'd accepted his offer of a brandy. 'Sheikh who?' she stuttered, as though it mattered. Any sheikh was as terrifying as any other.

He evidently caught her panic. Again he smiled, as the black eyes held hers. 'Catering for Arab princes, my dear Miss Copeland, is no different from catering for anyone else. Though there are a couple of points of etiquette that you would do well to bear in mind.' He paused and let his eyes trail over her—the firm, full breasts, the well-shaped thighs—then back to her flushed and irritated face.

'At all times, dress modestly,' he advised. 'No plunging necklines, no hiked-up hemlines, sleeves below the elbows if you possibly can.'

Giselle glared back at him. 'Should I wear a veil?' she suggested with sarcasm.

'That won't be necessary.' He looked amused. 'However, that hair of yours . . .' He shook his head ambiguously as he regarded her wild, bright, tawny mane. 'Pin it up under some kind of cap.' Before she could cut in, he carried on, a deliberately provocative edge to his voice. 'In some societies, you see, to see the hair of a female has historically been the privilege of the male who dominates her.' He paused, his eyes on her face. 'And you, if I may say so, have such extraordinarily beautiful hair.'

Just for a moment Giselle was speechless. She had been about to pounce on him and tear him apart for that shamelessly chauvinistic remark. The privilege of the male who dominates her, indeed! The very concept belonged to another century! And yet she had been abruptly stopped in her tracks by the unexpected compliment. Somehow, the look in his eyes as he had said it had sent a shiver down her spine.

She pulled herself together and responded tightly, 'I reckon you should have hired a man.'

'Not at all.' He dropped his eyes and drank. 'A woman in the role of provider of sustenance is much more appropriate, I believe. Besides,' he added quickly, as the anger flared in her eyes again and she opened her mouth to suggest that 'the role of servant' was what he'd really meant, 'I have total faith in your taste and decorum. I'm sure you would not wish to offend our Moslem brothers.'

When he put it like that, she could hardly dissent. 'I have no wish to offend anyone,' she assured him irritably.

'Good. Then there's no problem.' He leaned back his head and narrowed his eyes, regarding her closely from beneath long-lashed lids. 'And now for my second point . . . namely this.' He held up the glass of liquor in his hand. 'I shall have wine with my meal as usual, but kindly offer no alcohol to my guests. Just make sure there's plenty of mineral water on the table.' He paused. 'For the meal, serve anything you like. With the exception, of course, of pork or ham.'

Perhaps, Giselle was thinking crossly, she ought to invite him to make out a list. If there were any more rules and regulations to abide by perhaps he would like her to sit some kind of test! But he appeared, at least temporarily, to have run out of orders.

He laid aside his empty glass and moved on to a completely different subject. 'Was Ella here when you arrived?' he asked.

Giselle nodded. 'Yes,' she said.

'Did she show you round?'

'She showed me my room. I showed myself round after she'd left.'

The wide lips curved into a smile. 'I'm glad to hear it. I want you to make yourself at home here. Feel free to use anything—the video, the stereo—except when you have work to do, of course.' He held her eyes and smiled with faint humour that suggested she would have little time free from the responsibilities of work to indulge in such pastimes as movies and music. Then, glancing at his watch, he stirred and started to lean forward, pausing to put one final question to her before he rose. 'As I told you, I have some papers to deal with. Is there anything you would like to ask me before I leave you now?'

It was right on the tip of her tongue to say 'No' and it would undoubtedly have been more diplomatic if she had. She could see with her own eyes that he was desperately tired and unlikely to be in the mood for prying questions. But his reference to Ella had sharply reminded her of the girl's earlier, strangely unsettling revelation. She knew she would not rest in peace until she had confronted him with what she knew.

She took a deep breath and looked straight at him. 'Yes, there is, as a matter of fact.' Then, before her wavering courage deserted her, she swallowed and queried, as politely as she could, 'Why didn't you tell me you were married?'

He seemed to freeze before her eyes, the harsh, dark features turned to stone. 'Who,' he demanded in a low, threatening voice, 'have you been speaking to?'

Giselle felt a shiver run down her spine. The panther was looking ready to pounce—and more, eager to tear his victim apart. Nervously she swallowed again. 'Why need I have been speaking to anybody?' she challenged, taking refuge in evasion. 'The fact that a man has a wife isn't normally something he feels the need to hide.'

'So now you accuse me of deception!' The black eyes drove like skewers through her.

'Not exactly,' she protested. An affirmative answer, she sensed, would not be wise.

'Then what?'

She shrugged. 'A simple omission. I'm sure you intended to tell me eventually.'

'And why should I tell you about my private life? What possible business is it of yours?'

'It is if I'm living here!' she shot back

indignantly, suddenly feeling on surer ground. 'My staying here strikes me as slightly improper, considering you have a wife.'

The dark eyes narrowed. He leaned back in his seat. 'Slightly improper ... Is that what you think?' He smiled faintly at the notion. 'Perhaps, Miss Copeland, you are right. However ...' He paused and leaned back a little in his seat, for the moment suspending his attack. 'Whoever your informant was, their information was a little out of date. I no longer have a wife, Miss Copeland, only an ex-wife. We are divorced.'

'Divorced?'

'Divorced, Miss Copeland,' he repeated. Then he raised one coal-black eyebrow at her. 'I trust this additional information will allay your fears of impropriety?'

Giselle nodded. 'Of course.' Suddenly she felt faintly embarrassed for having raised the subject at all, even faintly apologetic for having accused him of deceit. Yet, at the same time, she felt strangely pleased to have had it confirmed that Davidian was unmarried. Simply for the sake of propriety, she hurried to assure herself. She had no other earthly interest in whether the wretched man was married or not!

That should have been the end of the conversation. She could sense he had no wish to pursue it. But, to her own slight surprise, she heard herself asking, 'Was she Lebanese too, your wife?'

A sharp, chilly silence swallowed the question. For a long, angry moment he said not a word. When he did speak his voice was low and flat, very carefully controlled. 'No, as a matter of fact, she was Brazilian. *Is* Brazilian, I should say.' The dark brow furrowed as he added softly, almost as though he was speaking to himself, 'We met while I was doing my postgraduate study at Harvard. Her father was a professor there. I was very young and impressionable.' He paused and shrugged. 'We both were, I guess.'

It was only the most fleeting of impressions, but, just for a moment, Giselle seemed to glimpse a new, unsuspected side of the man—open, compassionate, even vulnerable. A flash of something akin to humanity lightened the dark, forbidding eyes. Then, like a dream, it was instantly gone.

A shutter seemed to drop down over his eyes as he glanced down at his watch again. His lips thinned into a straight, tight line. The muscles around his jaw grew hard. 'And now, unless you have any more questions, I shall take my leave of you.' Interrogatively, he raised his eyes and awaited her response. His dark expression counselled her to answer in the negative.

Unhesitatingly, she obliged. 'I have no more questions.' Though that momentary lapse of his had made her curious. Was it possible, she was wondering, that the almighty, inscrutable Fayiz Davidian was prey to human emotions, after all?

If he was, he betrayed none now as, abruptly, he rose from his chair. His tone was detached and cutting as he told her, 'Good. In that case, I can get on with more important business.' He paused, then informed her, 'It is unlikely we shall see each other before tomorrow evening. I tend to leave rather early in the morning.' He flexed his shoulders tiredly and ran a hand across his thick dark hair. 'My guests are invited for eight o'clock. Kindly have dinner ready for nine.'

Then, without so much as a goodnight, he turned and walked swiftly from the room.

Giselle watched him go with a pang of unease and silently answered her own earlier question. That lapse of his had been totally misleading, and she had entirely misinterpreted what she had thought she had seen. The great Fayiz Davidian had no more capacity for human emotion than his brittly glittering crystal chandeliers.

No wonder his Brazilian wife had left him. What woman could live with a man like that?

She was up early next morning—though, as Davidian had predicted, he had already left. A man more single-mindedly devoted to his work would be very hard to find, she thought.

Ella was in the kitchen, polishing a pile of silver. She glanced up at Giselle with a friendly smile. 'Good morning. Did you sleep well?' she asked.

'Like a top.' Giselle crossed to the breakfast bar and helped herself to some orange juice—and it was just as she was hoisting herself up on to a stool that she noticed the note. A large white sheet of paper, folded in four and bearing her name. As, frowning, she began to open it up, Ella confirmed what she had already guessed.

'It's some instructions for the dinner tonight from Mr Davidian. A list of special Arab sweetmeats he wants you to get.' As Giselle stared down at the list of baffling names, written in a strong, bold hand, she added helpfully, 'Don't worry, I can tell you where to get them and how they should be served.'

'He says in this note that I also have to ask you to show me how to make special Arab coffee . . .' There was a faint note of dismay in her voice. Could it be, she was starting to think, that she had taken on more than she'd bargained for? Catering for Arab princes was perhaps not so straightforward, after all.

But the Filipino maid threw her a reassuring smile, 'No problem,' she protested. 'Ella will look after you!'

She did too. She showed her how to make the coffee, an aromatic brew flavoured with green cardamoms, advised her on the best local shops to do her shopping—'If you ever get stuck for anything, just pop into Harrods. They'll usually have it and they're just down the road!'—and patiently took time out before leaving at four to show her Davidian's preferred table settings.

As the French carriage clock in the dining-room struck a melodic half-past seven and Davidian came sweeping through the front door, it was thanks to Ella's invaluable co-operation that Giselle was feeling confidently in control.

Davidian immediately proceeded to pull the rug out from under her feet. 'Slight change of plan,' he told her casually, sticking his head round the dining-room door. 'There'll be one extra guest for dinner tonight. Set a separate table in the drawing-room.'

'You mean there'll be four of you? But I've only cooked for three!'

He shrugged unsympathetically and glanced at his watch. 'I'm sure you'll think of something, Miss Copeland.' Then he added, smiling an infuriating smile, 'And now please excuse me. I have to shower and change.'

Damn him! She glared at his retreating back. Couldn't he have phoned to let her know instead of saving up his little surprise until just half an hour before his guests were due? She flounced through to the kitchen to inspect the bubbling pots and pans. As long as this extra guest wasn't Desperate Dan, there should be plenty of food to go round; for safety's sake, she always cooked generous portions. But having to serve this extra person in a separate room from the rest of the guests would rather upset her presentation.

Bad-temperedly, she hurried through to the drawing-room and set up a little individual table. It was an odd request to make, she reflected. Why did this person have to eat separately? It must be some lower-class individual, some servant or the like, whose rank was not sufficiently exalted to befit them to dine at the same table as princes.

She scowled in silent disapproval. Well, whoever this lowly individual might be, she personally intended treating them with no less courtesy than she planned on treating the sheikhs!

The guests were invited for eight, Davidian had told her, yet eight o'clock came and went and there was no sign of them—or him. It was almost half past the hour when she heard him come unhurriedly along the corridor. At the sight of her faintly worried frown, he shook his head at her and smiled. 'Don't worry, they'll show up any minute now. Punctuality is not an Arab tradition. In the desert one measures time by days and hours, not minutes. Our obsession with such minute precision, to such people, seems unnatural and strange.'

As he spoke, his eyes swept over her, taking in the neat blue uniform, discreetly high-necked and down past her knees, and her modestly pinned-back hair beneath its starched white cap, and his approval was plainly written on his face. He smiled. 'I trust you managed your preparations without too many problems?'

She nodded, flushing, not quite certain why. 'Yes, thank you,' she answered. 'Ella gave me a helping hand.'

'Yes.' He continued to look down at her. 'She's a very sweet and obliging girl.'

He was wearing a slim, dark suit, broad-shouldered, double-breasted, with a soft silk shirt of purest white and a gold and crimson chequered tie. Against the lustrous white silk of his collar the black hair glistened like burnished ebony and the commanding lines of his olive-toned features—high brow, straight nose and wide, fine mouth—were sympathetically relaxed and softened for once. And the smile he was smiling seemed to reach right back into the depths of the deep velvet eyes.

As he reached out one hand to catch a loose tendril of her hair and softly curl it behind her ear, she caught the faintest heady tang of subtle, expensive aftershave. Some Eastern aphrodisiac, she wondered vaguely, aware that something had quickened her heartbeat.

As his fingers softly brushed her lobe, then paused to caress the soft skin of her throat, for a moment his gaze poured into her soul and she stared up at him, unresisting, entranced. The warmth of the soft dark skin against hers felt acutely intimate, yet oddly pleasurable. Then, just as he opened his mouth to speak, the doorbell rang and the moment was shattered.

'I'll get it.'

Instantly his hand dropped away and he was turning abruptly and heading for the hall. Giselle watched him go with a sense of confusion. How could she have just stood there and allowed him to touch her like that? This time the lapse had definitely been hers!

A moment later all such concerns were driven from her head as the front door opened and Sheikh Hamad and his brother Sheikh Abdulaziz came sweeping into the hall.

Two tall men in flowing Arab robes—the long white *dishdasha*, the immaculate headdress or *kaffiyeh* secured by its silken black tasselled cord and, over their shoulders, the gossamer *basht*, spun from finest camel hair and bordered with gold.

'*A'salam u'alaikum.*'

'*Wa' alaikum a'salam.*'

Giselle watched, enchanted by the spectacle, as warm but dignified greetings were exchanged. Then she felt her heart give a little leap as Davidian turned and beckoned to her. Surely she, a mere catering person, was not about to be introduced to the sheikhs?

She was absolutely right. She was not.

As she approached the group and Davidian instructed softly, 'Kindly accompany the sheikha to the drawing-room,' she felt a sharp sense of shock at the sight that met her eyes. A female figure she had not even noticed, draped from head to toe in a black *chaddor*. So this was the unexpected third guest who had been relegated to eat alone. Not some lowly servant at all, but a high-ranking sheikha, a low-ranking woman.

Without even glancing at Davidian or at either of the other two men, Giselle accompanied the tiny figure across the hallway to the empty drawing-room. As she bade her sit, she glanced at her curiously, wondering who she was. A wife? A daughter? It was hard to tell. All that was visible beneath the long black *chaddor* was a pair of tiny gold-slippered feet, though the heavily-ringed hands that clutched the veil around her throat were the soft, unmarked hands of a very young girl.

The girl sat without a word, her movements graceful and contained. 'Just make yourself at home,' Giselle urged kindly, feeling the girl's nervous sense of strangeness, wondering if she understood. Then, hearing the men move through to the reception room that adjoined the dining-room across the hallway, she glanced down quickly at her watch. She had twenty minutes to get the first course on the table. Almost apologetically, she headed for the door. 'I'll be back as soon as I can,' she promised.

She served the men first—Davidian would expect that—though it somewhat stuck in her craw to do so. Somehow this whole tawdry situation crystallised quite perfectly his attitude to women.

When she returned to the drawing-room the girl had shed her *chaddor* to reveal a shapely slender figure in a long red silk dress, her wrists and throat banded by gold and rubies, her black hair falling in cascades to her shoulders. She was beautiful, like some tiny, rare, exquisite bird. But as she cast a shy smile in Giselle's direction, Giselle felt her heart go out to her. Not for all the gold and rubies in the world would she have wished to change places with her.

In other respects, however, the evening proved most satisfactory. To Giselle's faintly grudging delight and relief, course after course was demolished with gusto. And, to her infinite surprise, her efforts were praised.

She had just finished serving the sweetmeats and coffee when Sheikh Hamad caught her eye. 'A very fine meal,' he told her, smiling. '*Shokrun*. We offer our thanks.'

Caught by surprise, Giselle hesitated for a moment, letting her eyes scan the forceful dark face of the man who was speaking to her. With its black moustache and large hooked nose, it was an autocratic face, but there was an unexpected spark of warmth in the dark brown eyes. Aware that Davidian was watching her closely, she returned the man's smile politely. 'Thank you, sir. I'm glad you enjoyed it.'

The guests left almost as soon as the coffee and sweetmeats had been cleared away. Giselle was in the drawing-room, folding away the sheikha's lonely little table, when Davidian appeared in the doorway. He had shed his jacket and loosened his tie. His hands were in his trouser pockets as he told her, 'Congratulations on another success. That was the best meal that's ever been served in this house.'

For some reason, the compliment only served to irritate her. She turned to face the tall, masculine figure, so poised, so privileged, so arrogantly sure of himself. 'Why was that poor girl not allowed to eat with the others?' she wanted to know.

At her abrasive tone, his expression hardened, but at least he offered an explanation of sorts. 'She is the daughter of Sheikh Hamad and betrothed to another man. The customs of her people forbid her to eat in the company of a man to whom she is not related. Myself, in this particular case.' He ground the words out like shards of shredded steel, then fixed her with a bayonet look. 'I trust that satisfies your curiosity on the matter?'

But his glib explanation, and his attitude, had only made her even angrier. 'And I suppose you approve of that sort of treatment?' she accused.

'Sexual apartheid, that's all it is!'

Fayiz took a step towards her. His features had darkened into a scowl. 'What I approve of and what goes on inside this house are none of your damned business,' he rasped. 'I pay you to cook for my guests, not to pass judgement on their lifestyles, or mine.' He towered over her, his anger tangible. 'Kindly remember that and stick to what concerns you.'

'Remember my place, you mean?' In spite of the menace that sparked from the dark eyes, Giselle could not restrain her own indignation. Fearlessly she thrust her jaw at him. 'Because of my doubly lowly position as a humble employee and a woman, am I supposed not to have the right to express an opinion? Is that what you're trying to tell me?'

'That's exactly what I'm trying to tell you. You see, I couldn't be less interested in your damned opinion!'

'I'll bet! I doubt you've ever listened to a female opinion in your life! Little wonder your wife walked out on you!'

It was out before she could bite it back. For a long, excruciating moment he said not a word, just looked at her as though he might devour her. 'What did you say?' he growled at her menacingly.

Unnerved, she took a step back. 'Nothing,' she defended. 'I was just suggesting that your relationships with women perhaps leave a little to be desired.'

She would have done better to have remained

silent. Vengeance joined forces with the anger in his face, and before she could move out of his way he had reached out roughly and grabbed hold of her. Fingers of steel clamped round her arms, totally immobilising her, digging into her flesh. And as he jerked her to him, like a rag doll, so that the heat of anger in him seemed to scorch right through to her bones, she felt her heart give a sickening lurch.

For suddenly she was remembering, all too clearly, his warning about the dangers of playing with fire . . .

CHAPTER FIVE

'LET ME GO! I didn't mean . . .! You have no right!' Giselle's protests came out in a garbled babble, her tongue tripping clumsily over the words as she struggled to free herself from his grasp. All she could see were the burning black eyes that drove right through her like merciless skewers, and all too clearly she could read the chilling message written there.

'I warned you . . .!'

She shivered as he ground the words at her, her stomach clenching in a knot of cold fear. As his grip around her body tightened, cruel fingers digging into her flesh, paralysed, she held her breath and waited, as defenceless as a rabbit in a panther's paw.

The hard, broad chest was pressed against her and the heat of his hands was in her hair, as roughly he snatched the lace cap from her head, so that her bright tresses fell down round her face. He pushed them back, the dark eyes blazing, his voice raw and husky as he told her, 'You want to know about my relationships with women? Allow me to give you a practical demonstration!'

'No, no! Let me go!' Overcome by a sudden fierce panic, Giselle tried to snatch her head away. Defensively, she stiffened and strained away from him, every atom of her strength concentrated on breaking free.

But she was no match for his power or the ruthless purpose that smouldered in the dark coals of his eyes. Impatiently he jerked her closer, imprisoning her within his arms, then twisted her head round once more to face him, as he persuaded in a low, throaty growl, 'Come, *habibiti*. Relax.' A ferocious dark smile touched his lips. 'Why not just surrender and enjoy the little lesson you're about to receive? I can satisfy much more than your curiosity if you'll just stop fighting and give me a chance.'

All at once Giselle's stomach was churning. Anxiety throbbed deep in her throat. All her puny efforts to resist him were making absolutely no impact at all. As the hard wall of his chest crushed against her breasts, she heard herself gabble, 'No! Please! Don't do this to me!' But her protests were abruptly silenced as his mouth ground down savagely on hers.

If this was a mere clinical demonstration, she found herself wondering in muzzy confusion, as the burning heat of his lips consumed her, then what must it feel like to be kissed by this man when his heart and soul were also involved? Like being consumed by a volcano, she could but dimly, helplessly surmise, as her flesh seemed to melt beneath the onslaught and the blood in her veins burst into flames.

For, as passionately as she had initially resisted, she now found herself responding to him.

The throbbing animal heat of his body that

pressed hungrily against her own ignited her nerve-ends like a torch to a cannon, sending wild sensations exploding through her veins. As his hands moved possessively over her back and shoulders, exploring every dip and curve, then upwards with long, strong fingers to sweep through the tangled mane of her hair, with a shudder of yearning she leaned against him, her body limp and filled with desire, her senses alive and glowing greedily beneath the voluptuous sensuality of his caress.

'Is this what you wanted to know, *habibiti*?' Without mercy, his eyes burned down into hers, then impatiently he was pulling her to him again, his hard hot mouth devouring hers, sharp teeth biting against her lip, as he invaded her greedily with his tongue. 'Is it?' he insisted roughly, as one hand swept round to possess her breast, his touch sending ricochets of burning sensation coursing through her throbbing veins. 'Tell me, my dear Giselle, does this answer your question for you? Or is there more you'd like to know?'

Giselle gasped and shuddered as his hand moved against her, caressing rhythmically with his open palm, a leisurely, expert, erotic caress. And with a flush of shame, she felt herself press against him as her loins filled with a sudden unutterable longing for his total, consuming possession of her.

For one bright sharp moment of utter abandon she almost longed to cry out and beg him to take her. Never had she felt any yearning so keenly. Her whole being was consumed with it.

But all at once his hands had grown still and his bruising lips had abandoned hers. He stepped back, releasing her, and regarded her coldly, a look of frozen contempt on his face. 'Now you know something of my relations with women—and whether or not they leave something to be desired!'

It was almost as though he had spat in her face. Shocked, Giselle felt herself blanche and freeze. Then, as he continued to gaze down on her with dark detachment, she was stepping backwards, hastily, away from him, struggling to regain some small fragment of composure.

Yet in spite of the upheaval that raged within her—her heart was still racing, her limbs turned to powder—she forced herself to shoot right back at him with all the scorn that she could muster, 'I reckon I understand all too perfectly about the nature of your relations with women! To you they're nothing but sex objects. Sex objects or servants!'

Lazily, his eyes trailed over her. 'And which of these two particular functions are you complaining about? I would suggest it's not the former.' He eyed her flushed face, her tousled hair, the still excited panting of her dishevelled bosom. 'From that remarkable little demonstration you just gave me, it seems to me that, like most women, you really quite enjoy being treated as a sex object.'

Damned chauvinist! Of course he'd think that! 'Well, you're wrong!' Giselle defended, glaring back at him, hating him with a deep, dark fury. 'Though I know only too well that it would be a waste of time trying to convince a blinkered chauvinist like you!' As though in practical support of that theory she swung away stiffly and headed for the door. 'A man with your mediaeval turn of mind isn't worth wasting time and energy on!'

Fayiz watched her retreating back with a slow smile on his lips. Ignoring her outburst, he threw an offer after her, his tone scathing and deliberately provocative. 'Remember, if you have any more queries at all about how I relate to women, please don't be shy, feel free to ask. I'd be more than happy to supply you with a more comprehensive demonstration—anywhere, any time.'

At the door, Giselle paused and threw him a black look. 'Please don't hold your breath!' she scorned. 'I already know all I need to know—and I find every bit of it contemptible!'

But as she swung away into the hall, aware of the taunting dark eyes that followed her, she felt a stab of discomfort prick her soul. If only the truth were really that simple!

The following few weeks were every bit as busy as Fayiz had warned her they would be. Virtually every evening there were clients to entertain, and on the occasional evening when she was free Giselle was really much too exhausted to do anything other than watch TV or sleep.

But she found unexpected satisfaction, even pleasure, in the challenge of trying to keep up with Davidian's punishing schedule. And she couldn't help but be both intrigued and entertained by the constant stream of colourful visitors to the Belgravia flat. The company of Arab princes—and the occasional lonely sheikha—was becoming almost a commonplace in her life. She no longer felt awkward or intimidated in their presence. And her ear was even growing accustomed to the guttural melodiousness of their strange tongue.

As far as Fayiz was concerned, she had had no more unfortunate brushes with him.

To her relief, it was only on very rare occasions that she found herself alone in his company. On the evenings when there were guests he would retire to his room as soon as they had left, and on the occasional evening when there were none, though he had never told her what he did or where he went, she suspected he stayed on to work late at the office. She would hear him return as she was preparing for bed, and once, after dozing off in the middle of a video, she observed on her way back to her own room that the light in his room still burned brightly, though it was already after one o'clock.

What drove him to work so relentlessly? she found herself wondering with a curious pang, observing next day how exhausted he looked. Surely he didn't need to? Was it simply greed for more riches, or what?

Whatever the reason, she did not burden herself unduly with wondering. If it was Fayiz Davidian's intention to work himself into an early grave, that was entirely up to him. For her part, she simply felt relieved that his pathological attachment to his work kept him conveniently out of her hair. Thanks to his absence for most of the time, her stay at the flat was proving quite agreeable.

She might have known such tranquillity could not last.

It was Ella who gave her the first indication that some change in her civilised routine was afoot, as Giselle helped herself to breakfast one Thursday morning.

'Mr Davidian told me to tell you that he wants a word with you when he gets back this evening.' The pretty Filipino girl glanced up from her ironing and threw her Titian-haired friend a wink. 'I got the impression it was something important.'

Giselle bit sharply into her toast. 'No doubt he's planning to spring some surprise on me, like a dinner party for fifty tomorrow night!' She grimaced elaborately and groaned, aware that the remark was only half in jest. After all, wasn't that precisely the sort of trick that Davidian would take sadistic pleasure in pulling?

Ella smiled sympathetically, but said nothing, and Giselle resisted a fleeting temptation to quiz her. Since that mild indiscretion on the day of Giselle's arrival, when she had mentioned the existence of a Mrs Davidian, on the subject of her employer and his personal business, the otherwise open and co-operative Ella had become as tight as a clam.

Whether Davidian had warned her—a distinct possibility—or whether she was simply acting on her own careful wisdom, the upshot was exactly the same. It was a total waste of time Giselle asking any questions. They would simply be met with an eloquent shrug and the inevitable answer, 'I really don't know.'

And who could blame her? Giselle thought without rancour. Ella had a permanent job to hold down. Unlike herself, the dutiful Filipino girl would still be working for Davidian in two months' time.

So, as far as this evening and what Davidian had in store for her was concerned, Giselle would just have to wait and see.

In spite of the fact that there was no dinner party that evening, Giselle was extremely busy all day. In the morning she shopped for things for the freezer and then spent the entire afternoon preparing enormous quantities, also for the freezer, of an exotic meringue and chocolate pudding that had found particular favour with Davidian's guests.

One of her own favourites too, it demanded painstaking preparations—not the sort of thing you could whip up in an hour—though Davidian had demanded its inclusion in the menu more than once at very short notice. After the chaos of the first time, when she had only just made it, she had prudently resolved never to be caught out again.

Just after six she had finally finished and hurriedly started clearing up the kitchen. She would have a quick shower and change, she decided, and be ready for Davidian coming home. If he had something of importance to tell her, there was a good chance that he would be home at a decent hour.

She might have known better, she concluded wearily, as at eight forty-five there was still no sign of him. She finished off the fish dish she had prepared for supper and stacked her dirty dishes in the dishwasher. Then she poured herself coffee and went through to the TV room. She would watch the news and then a movie—at least for as long as she could stay awake. Then, whether Davidian had turned up or not, she would take herself off, deservedly, to bed.

Just after eleven her eyelids began drooping. She sighed. It was time to call it a day. She flicked off the TV and uncurled slowly from the comfort of the deep, soft claret armchair. If Davidian was annoyed that she hadn't waited, that was really just too bad. It was her job to cope with all the work he could throw at her, but it was not in her contract to be his personal doormat!

Pleased with herself for making this gesture—let him treat her in future a little more considerately!—she washed quickly and changed into her frilly white nightgown, the one with the delicate shoestring straps and the daring side slashes from thigh to ankle. Then with a sigh of anticipation she climbed between the sheets and stretched out to switch off the bedside lamp. For once, a reasonably early night. Sheer luxury! It was precisely what she needed.

As her head sank blissfully into the pillows a feeling of delicious drowsiness washed over her.

With a sigh of contentment she closed her eyes and waited for blessed sleep to claim her.

But what felt like but a moment later she was rudely and unceremoniously awakened.

At first she thought she must be dreaming, but the sudden harsh light that shone in her eyes was much too vivid for a dream. And the deep, peremptory tones that assailed her ears were all too familiarly of the waking world. She sat up with a start, her eyes blinking open, her heart jumping in her chest at the sight before her.

'I thought I left a message that I wanted to speak to you? What's the matter, *habibiti*, did you conveniently forget?'

He was standing in the doorway, one hand still on the light switch, a dark angry figure in a charcoal-grey suit. The black brows were knitted in intense irritation and the set of the strong wide jaw was ferocious. And, though he looked as though he might demolish her if she provoked him, Giselle couldn't resist answering in a flat, accusing tone,

'No, as a matter of fact, I didn't forget. I simply grew tired of waiting, that's all.'

'Did you, *habibiti*? Did you indeed?' The words ground from his lips like sharded steel. 'Well, lest you make the same mistake again, let me point out to you, unequivocally, that when I ask you to wait up for me you'll damn well do it!'

All drowsiness had slipped abruptly away from her. The adrenalin of anger was rushing through her veins. How dared he speak to her in this imperious fashion, like some Eastern potentate addressing a slave? With a proud, imperious gesture of her own, she thrust back the bedclothes and swung her feet to the floor to stand before him in angry splendour, a picture of perfect quivering defiance.

'I'll damn well do nothing of the sort! If you want to speak to me you should get in at a decent hour. I'm not your lackey, Fayiz Davidian! Let's be very clear about that!'

In the overpowering thrall of her outrage she had momentarily forgotten her scanty attire. If he had not smiled then and let his dark eyes slide over her—'How magnificent you are when you're aroused . . .'—she might have continued to be innocently unconscious of the splendidly alluring spectacle she presented to his eyes. For the thin silky shoulder straps of her nightdress had slipped revealingly halfway down her arms, while the generously slashed side seams clung provocatively to her thighs.

She felt his gaze drift down like a soft caress to the swell of her indignantly heaving breasts, lingering for a moment on the smooth creamy flesh, and, just for a moment, inwardly, she froze. Dear lord, she was standing here half naked before him and he was shamelessly lapping up the spectacle!

Giselle fought back the blush that rose up from her toes and only just managed to resist the temptation to turn and dive in panic beneath the bedclothes. That was no way to behave. At all costs she must retain her dignity.

With commendable poise, looking him straight in the eye, she adjusted her shoulder straps and pointed behind him. 'Please be so kind as to pass me my robe. It's on the hook on the back of the door.'

With a quirk of amusement Fayiz obeyed and held out the demure towelling garment for her to slip into. 'You really needn't bother on my account. I find you perfectly acceptable as you are.'

Of course he would, shameless lecher that he was!

Turning her back on him, Giselle thrust her arms into the sleeves of the robe, careful to avoid any contact with his fingers, then abruptly snatched the front closed around her and secured the belt tightly about her slim waist. Then, feeling decidedly less vulnerable, she turned once more to face him, a flash of righteous anger burning in her eyes. 'So what's so important,' she demanded, 'that you felt obliged to take the liberty of barging in here?' The tightness of her lips accused him. 'I suppose you know you had no right to do that?'

Characteristically, he seemed to be thoroughly uninterested in debating the rights or wrongs of his actions. Treating her demand as though it had never been spoken, he crossed to one of the blue upholstered bedroom chairs and, loosening his tie, lowered his tall frame on to it. 'Why did you go to bed,' he enquired curtly, 'when you had been informed by Ella that I wanted to speak to you?'

Giselle glowered down at him, loathing his

arrogance. 'I was tired,' she answered, equally curtly. 'You may have conveniently forgotten, but I didn't finish working until after midnight last night.'

Fayiz surveyed her coolly, as his long bronzed fingers fiddled to undo the top button of his shirt. 'Is that so, *habibiti*?' he purred in answer. Then as he paused, still looking up at her, she fully expected that he would go on to point out that that was no great sacrifice. Didn't he habitually work till long after midnight? But she had forgotten that Fayiz rarely said what she expected, and she was mildly surprised when he observed, 'Is the pace too much for you, *habibiti*?' His tone was scathing. 'Are you cracking up already beneath the pressure?'

That suggestion put her instantly on the defensive. He had the infuriating knack of doing that as well. She straightened irritably and shot back almost rudely, 'As a matter of fact, I'm not, *habibiti*. I can keep pace with anything you care to throw at me!'

For a moment, the gold and the jet eyes locked. The air between them seemed to shimmer. Then, all at once, quite unexpectedly, Fayiz's dark expression softened. '*Habibi*, not *habibiti*,' he corrected her with that quirk of a smile that so characterised his change of humour. 'If you insist on offering me endearments in Arabic, you must get your genders right. *Habibiti* is the female form of "my dear". *Habibi* is the form one would use to a man.'

Giselle glared at him mutely for a moment. No

desire could be further from her heart than offering endearments to Fayiz Davidian in Arabic, or in any other language, come to that! 'My mistake,' she offered through her teeth. 'I was under the impression that it was a form of abuse.'

'Far from it, *jamila* Giselle.' He smiled a wicked smile, deliberately confounding her, and leaned back a little in his chair, letting his eyes travel over her in languid appreciation. 'Surely you could not seriously have imagined that I would use abusive language to one as lovely as yourself? That would be a most ungentlemanly thing to do.' Then his eyes stayed on her as he added, 'Why don't you sit down and make yourself comfortable? I'm getting a terrible crick in the back of my neck having to look up at you all the time!'

That was the first bit of good news she'd had since he'd wakened her. She straightened her shoulders and glared straight back at him with not the remotest intention of sitting down. Let his damned neck break for all she cared! 'I'd rather you just got on and said what you came to say. I'd like to get back to bed and get some sleep.'

Fayiz flexed his shoulders and stretched his long legs out in front of him. 'Forgive me,' he entreated with more sarcasm than remorse, 'for being so inconsiderate as to keep you from your beauty sleep.' He let his eyes drift up once more to her face. 'If you had waited up for me, as I requested, we could have made this encounter a whole lot briefer.'

Giselle clenched her fists and did not answer. It

would only encourage him in his perversity to drag the interview out even longer. He was already, she sensed, meeting his implacable black gaze, taking considerable pleasure in doing just that.

Almost as though testing her self-control, he deliberately took his time about answering. Then, with infuriating calm, he told her, 'We're going down to Chiltham Hall for the weekend. I want you to be ready and packed by three tomorrow. We'll be returning to London on Sunday evening.'

In a flash of panic Giselle instantly remembered her earlier jest to Ella about a dinner party for fifty. Fingers crossed mentally, she requested, 'Does that mean you'll be entertaining over the weekend?'

Fayiz smiled at her strangely. 'In a sense.'

'In what sense?' She waited for clarification. He was deliberately being obscure.

'There will be no dinner parties for clients. Just one young lady to provide for.'

'Not a client?'

'Not a client.' The black eyes twinkled.

'A friend, perhaps?'

'A little more than a friend.'

'I see.' Giselle's lips tightened disapprovingly. He was planning a weekend with one of his baubles! 'In that case, I can't see why you need me along. It is not my duty to cater for your lady-friends.'

He responded at once to the sharpness of her tone with a sudden overriding sharpness of his own. 'It is your duty to do whatever I tell you. And I am telling you you will be accompanying me down to

Kent tomorrow. Your duties will be explained to you when we get there—and there will be no further discussion on that point.' He held her eyes, daring her to argue, and all at once Giselle just had to retaliate.

Throwing caution to the winds, she informed him disparagingly, 'Don't worry, I shall do my duty—but I can't help wondering about this female friend of yours. The woman must be a raving masochist to want to have anything to do with you!'

'You think so?' To her surprise there was no anger in the question, just a tinge òf superior amusement. 'Apparently, then, there is no shortage of raving masochists amongst the female sex. Fortunately I have never encountered the slightest problem when recruiting female company.'

Giselle didn't doubt that that was true. A man with the fatal good looks and worldly poise—not to mention the inordinate wealth—that Fayiz Davidian possessed would have no trouble at all in 'recruiting' virtually any female who had the misfortune to catch his eye. But any woman who continued to stick around after she'd had a chance to see behind the façade, in Giselle's estimation, had to be seriously mad. With a toss of her head, she told him so. 'I suppose that that just goes to show how totally undiscerning some women are.'

'I suppose it does.' He smiled again, apparently still more amused than irritated by her attack. 'But then, as I've pointed out before, women are an unstable, unreliable breed. Who knows what strange logic drives them? Not me, that's for sure.'

Nor, Giselle observed to herself, as slowly now he started to stand up, would he be interested in finding out. As long as women continued to serve what purpose he required of them—as passive sex objects and servants—he would not be the least bit interested in uncovering the complexities of the female psyche.

He stood before her, making her wish she had sat down, and for one tantalising moment held her eyes. Then he leaned, unexpectedly, to kiss her on the cheek. 'I look forward to our weekend together.'

Then, leaving her to ponder exactly what he meant by that, he turned away quickly and left the room.

CHAPTER SIX

THE three prearranged sharp bursts on the doorbell, announcing Fayiz's arrival downstairs to collect her, sounded at precisely one minute to three. Giselle grabbed her suitcase and headed through the front door, marvelling at the precision of his punctuality. The man functioned with the accuracy of a computer. No tardy son of the desert he!

The passenger door of the white Mercedes swung open the moment she stepped on to the pavement. Then in a flash of efficiency he was round beside her, taking instant charge of her battered old suitcase and stowing it swiftly alongside his own in the trunk.

'Just one more thing.' As he climbed in beside her, he reached for the car phone and switched it off. 'The weekend starts here.' He threw her a wink. 'No more business calls for the next forty-eight hours!'

Giselle could scarcely believe her eyes and ears. She lifted one approving but sceptical eyebrow. 'I'm glad to see you take your pleasures seriously. This lady-friend of yours must be pretty special.'

'Indeed she is.' He tossed her a smug smile as the big car started to move away. 'These weekends of ours mean a very great deal to me.'

Giselle regarded him with a flicker of suspicion. There was something strange and different about him today, a new dimension in his manner that she had never glimpsed before—an air of eagerness and excitement that was almost boyishly disarming. And barely a glimmer of the harsh and worldly Fayiz whom she had come to know.

Ah, well, even Genghis Khan, presumably, had had his human side, she conceded. The prospect of a weekend in the eager arms of one of his compliant female baubles was evidently doing him a power of good. Though she cynically doubted that there was any real depth to this sudden display of human frailty. Whatever emotions had taken a hold of him would not have touched his heart, only his hormones.

Even as that disparaging thought formed within her, her eyes drifted unbidden to the well-shaped fingers that lightly yet somehow sensuously manipulated the steering wheel. And in spite of herself she could not help recalling how those fingers had felt against her skin.

She swallowed drily and drew back in her seat as her body stirred with a sudden secret pleasure, and, very deliberately, she averted her eyes. In spite of the powerful way he moved her, not for all the tea in China would she change places with this weekend bauble of his. Not for all the gold and rubies of the Orient, she chided herself further, upping the stakes. He might be capable of showing little glimpses of heaven through those seductive hands and lips of his, but a meaningless and dispensable bauble was all any woman would ever be to him.

And though her own treacherous body secretly burned for him, she knew she could never allow herself to be treated as a bauble by any man. Unlike all those other women in his life, she was definitely no raving masochist!

They reached Chiltham Hall just before four-thirty and scrunched to a halt on the wide gravel forecourt. Then, with impatience in his every gesture, Fayiz was grabbing their cases from the car boot and hurrying up the stone staircase to the front door.

'Mrs Pennygreen will show you to your room,' he informed Giselle brusquely over his shoulder. Then, with a quick glance at his watch, he was hurrying through the front door and across the huge hall towards the stairs. 'I'm just going to have a very quick shower.'

Such unabashed keenness! Giselle thought with a twist, observing how he took the stairs two at a time. Such single-minded anticipation! He must, after all, be in serious need of this weekend!

Mrs Pennygreen seemed pleased to see her as she showed her upstairs to her room—an exceedingly pretty room in shades of rose, with, of course, the inevitable ensuite bathroom.

'How are you enjoying life in London?' she enquired as they made their way back downstairs again. 'Is Mr Davidian keeping you busy?'

'You can say that again!' Giselle laughed in confirmation. 'But I like hard work. I'm really quite enjoying it.'

The plump-faced woman touched her arm. 'I was grateful when Mr Davidian told me that you'd offered to give me a hand this weekend. That was really very kind of you, my dear.'

'I'm only too glad to give you a hand,' Giselle quickly assured her with total sincerity, yet remembering with an inward flash of anger the manner in which her presence here had been commandeered. The pressure he had put on her had been quite unnecessary, if all she was here for was to give Mrs Pennygreen a hand. All he'd had to do was ask her. She would have been happy to oblige.

Had he been unaware of that, she wondered, or was it simply, as she suspected, that he was addicted to throwing his weight around?

Unaware of these mental machinations, Mrs Pennygreen was smiling at her. 'These weekends are always a little hectic, and I'm not as fit as I used to be.'

Giselle managed to squeeze back a smile in response, camouflaging her disapproval. Hectic indeed! She could well believe it—even picture it in glorious Technicolor as she gave unlicensed rein to her imagination.

Breakfasts in bed, midnight champagne, seductive, candlelit dinners for two with oysters and soft music and all manner of aphrodisiacs. Mentally, she sniffed and tossed her head. Well, personally she would be damned if she would aid and abet such displays of shameless fleshly indulgence. If Fayiz and his lady friend wanted breakfast in bed, or champagne, or oysters, or anything else, they could darned well get it for themselves!

Just at that moment the entryphone buzzed and with a quick glance at Giselle Mrs Pennygreen hurried to answer it. 'That'll be the young lady,' she observed with a wink.

Her prediction was instantly confirmed. With a broad smile the housekeeper replaced the entryphone receiver and picked up the internal phone at its side. She punched in a number—Fayiz's bedroom, Giselle guessed—then announced in warm tones, 'She's on her way, sir.'

Giselle's immediate instinct was to withdraw. It wasn't her place to stick around for the imminent grand arrival, and to be perfectly honest she had no desire to. For, suddenly, the thought of meeting Fayiz's lady-friend filled her with an acute, almost painful discomfort. A pulse in her throat had started nervously ticking and the palms of her hands felt clammy and damp. It made no sense that she should feel so strongly, yet all at once she longed, quite desperately, to escape.

But even as she signalled her intention to retire diplomatically to the kitchen, Mrs Pennygreen shook her head. 'No, stay, Giselle,' she commanded firmly. 'I'm sure Mr Davidian would want you to.'

Giselle started to protest—'I really don't think so'—but was interrupted as Fayiz came hurrying down the stairs, dressed now not in his familiar City suit but in cotton drill trousers and a blue polo shirt. To her utter astonishment, he gestured to her to follow him. 'Come, Giselle. Come with me.'

Was he expecting her to carry the woman's bags or perhaps to bow her up the stairs to the house? Giselle wondered resentfully as she did as he had bade. If he expected either, he would be disappointed. As she had warned him once before, she was nobody's lackey.

But that, apparently, was not his intention. As, on dragging footsteps, she followed him outside, he gestured to her to wait at the top of the steps. Then, before she could nod, he was more than halfway down, taking the stone steps three at a time. He reached the lower gravelled forecourt in the very same instant that a gleaming black Bentley with mysteriously tinted windows emerged in stately splendour from the trees.

Giselle watched with ever-increasing anxiety, as the big car came to a whispering halt and, before the chauffeur had time to preside, Fayiz himself snatched open the rear door and leaned impatiently inside.

A moment later there was a squeal of pleasure and a warm dark burst of masculine laughter as Fayiz's head once more emerged with a pair of arms wrapped round his neck.

Instantly the tension in Giselle dissolved, to be replaced by a new, unexpected sense of wonder. Her eyes widened in astonishment, then she started to smile, as her mind and her eyes absorbed the sight before her. It was no less than a total revelation—though, something told her, she really should have guessed.

For the tiny, beautiful creature with the bright laughing face who was being held aloft in Fayiz's arms was, at a guess, no more than four years old!

It had to be his daughter. There could be no mistake. For even from the top of the steps Giselle could make out the startling likeness between the tiny, delicate dark-haired child and the equally dark-haired, broad-shouldered man. And there was an air of commonality about them that went far beyond mere similarities of colouring. A shared spirit, Giselle sensed. A common understanding. And, what was even more vividly and dramatically apparent, an overpowering exchange of love.

With a sublime smile Fayiz came up the steps, the child still held tightly in his arms. Then as Giselle went to meet them, wondering at the sight—rarely had she witnessed such an intense glow of happiness shining from a pair of human eyes—Fayiz lowered his daughter to the ground and squatted down on his haunches beside her.

'Rasha, say hello to Giselle,' he instructed. 'She'll be staying with us this weekend.'

Obediently the child looked up at Giselle, her dark eyes solemn as she held out her hand. 'Hello, Giselle. Papa told me about you.'

Did he indeed? Giselle hid her surprise, as she took the tiny hand in her own. 'I'm very pleased to meet you, Rasha. Rasha—that's a lovely name.'

'It means little deer.' The child looked proud. 'Papa says that when I was born I looked just like a baby deer.'

With those huge translucent long-lashed eyes that dominated her tiny face, Giselle could easily appreciate that that must indeed have been the case. She was about to say so, but stopped short as she realised that the little girl's attention was focused once more on her father.

'Can I go up to my room and change?' Rasha indicated, with a curl of her nose, the elaborately pin-tucked dress she was wearing. 'I want to go and play in the garden.'

'Good idea,' Fayiz agreed. 'Do you want me to go with you, or shall I wait for you down here?'

With no hesitation the child reached for his hand and tugged him behind her as she headed indoors. 'You come with me, Papa,' she demanded. 'I want you to help me choose.'

'And what about Giselle? I think she should come too. You can show her all your pretty clothes.'

Rasha paused politely, but, before she could answer, Giselle diplomatically intervened. 'Actually, I haven't finished unpacking yet. Perhaps you can show me your things tomorrow?' She could sense that right now her presence was superfluous. Rasha, quite clearly, wanted her father to herself, and Fayiz, she suspected, probably felt the same.

He certainly made no further effort to persuade her. 'OK, then,' he nodded. 'We'll see you later.' Then he was being propelled by a determined four-year-old across the hallway towards the staircase, Giselle watching their progress with a wry, bemused smile.

This was one spectacle she had never thought to witness—Fayiz Davidian at the mercy of a female! For there was no doubt that little Rasha had achieved what no female before her probably ever had. She had succeeded in wrapping the world's number one woman-hater like a piece of twine around her little finger!

The proximity of his little daughter clearly had a mellowing effect on Fayiz. Even after Rasha was tucked up in bed and Giselle, to her surprise, had been invited to join him for dinner—a meal which had been prepared in advance by Mrs Pennygreen—his new benevolently easy-going mood stayed with him.

'Join me for a brandy,' he invited, after he had helped her to clear away the dinner things. 'Come. Let's go through to the drawing-room.'

It couldn't last, of course, Giselle was thinking, as she made herself comfortable in one of the soft leather armchairs, arranging the skirt of her shirtdress over her knees. Right now the panther was behaving like a pussycat—barely a sign of tooth or claw—but the transformation was only temporary. As soon as the spell of his daughter wore off—or sooner, if Giselle were to make some wrong move—he would return to his familiar hardbitten self.

Still, relax and enjoy it while it lasts, she told herself cynically as he came towards her carrying two brandy glasses aloft. It isn't every day that one has the occasion to witness a real-life Hyde to Jekyll transformation!

He handed her her glass and sat down opposite her with a smile that would have outcharmed any Dr Jekyll. Then he leaned back a little, stretched his legs out in front of him and looked across at her with a smile in his eyes.

'So, what do you think of my daughter?' he

enquired.

'I think she's adorable,' Giselle answered frankly. 'You have every reason to be very proud of her.'

'Oh, I am,' he assured her, quite unnecessarily. Hadn't she seen ample evidence of that all evening? He took a mouthful of his cognac and savoured it before adding, 'And I'm going to be even more proud as she grows older. Rasha, I promise you, will achieve great things.'

Giselle tilted a frankly surprised eyebrow at him. 'Oh?' she enquired. 'What sort of things?'

Fayiz shrugged and loosened the tie at his throat, then slipped off the jacket of the light grey suit he had earlier changed into for dinner. 'That is something outside my power to tell you. Precisely where her ambitions lie must in time be decided by Rasha.'

He paused and gazed into the balloon-shaped brandy glass, almost as though consulting a crystal ball. Then, evidently pleased by what he saw there, he nodded confidently and carried on, 'All I can tell you, as her father, is that she will be given every advantage and opportunity that it is within my power to grant her. And I know she has it in her to do well. She's already the brightest child by far in her kindergarten class.'

Giselle smiled back at him, genuinely touched at the simplicity of his faith in the child and at the love he so obviously felt for her, though inwardly she could not suppress a frown at the blatant incongruity. That an out-and-out chauvinist like

Fayiz Davidian, a man who consistently referred
to women as that 'unreliable and unstable breed',
should identify so closely with a mere girl was
surely something of a contradiction? That he
should feel such pride and attachment for a
son—that was something she could have
understood more easily—but that he should so
obviously feel it for a daughter struck her as
unexpected to say the least.

At the risk of antagonising him, she had to say
so. In as mild a tone as she could muster, she gave
cautious voice to her surprise. 'Perhaps I'm wrong,
but I was under the impression that women in your
society don't count for very much?'

There was a heartbeat of silence, a subtle change
in the mood, as Fayiz laid his brandy glass aside.
'*My* society?' There was an edge to his voice, but
less of an edge than Giselle had expected. 'And to
which society do you assign me? Pray enlighten
me, *jamila* Giselle?'

'Middle Eastern society.' She met the dark gaze.
'That is, is it not, the society to which you belong?'

'Indeed it is. But Middle Eastern society is as
diverse and varied as the societies of Europe. I had
the good fortune to be born into one of the more
liberal Middle Eastern societies, as it happens, not
one of the more reactionary to which you seem to
refer.'

'Is that so? Well, on the whole, I'd say it doesn't
tend to show.' Having been rash enough to put
herself out on a limb, she was determined now to
defend her position. She looked him straight in the

eye. 'From what I've observed you seem quite happy to accommodate more reactionary points of view.'

She did not elaborate. He would know what she meant. And he did, at once. 'You mean the sheikhas?'

Giselle nodded. 'Precisely. If you were really so liberal you wouldn't stand for the way they're forced to eat separately.'

His eyes seemed to narrow. His lips thinned a little. He looked straight back at her without a flicker. 'And what would I do if I were really so liberal? Would I force my opinions on those who do not share them?' He paused a brief and scathing moment. 'That is not my definition of liberal, I'm afraid.' Then, before she could answer, he carried on, his tone controlled but nevertheless biting,

'The difference between you and me, *habibiti*, is that my experience over the years has taught me tolerance for other people's ways of life. I may not necessarily believe as they do, but I would defend their right to hold their own points of view.'

Beneath his calm appraisal Giselle squirmed a little. He was making her out to be some kind of bigot, and that cap most certainly did not fit. 'Some things are just wrong,' she insisted sharply. 'You can't defend them. Nobody can.'

His reaction surprised her. 'Of course. I agree. There are some things in this world that cannot be defended and it is our duty to resist them wherever we can. But there are, likewise, many areas of grey where right and wrong are not so easily identified. And what right have the likes of you and me to go insisting to an entire society that what they believe is wrong and what we believe is right? Why, when they have held such beliefs for centuries, should they even listen to such arrogance?'

Why indeed? All too clearly she could see his logic—but she wasn't about to admit that to him. 'So you just do nothing and go along with them? That doesn't strike me as a very honourable position.'

'Who said I do nothing?' He smiled at her thinly. 'I wage my own private war against injustice with the weapons of persuasion and example. It is not always necessary to go in with all guns blazing in order to exert a positive influence.'

'I realise that.' Giselle felt severely chastened. Perhaps he was more liberal than she had given him credit for.

'In the case of Rasha—' he held her eyes, as he returned to the subject that had sparked off the debate '—I am simply following the example that was passed down to me by my father. It was his greatest pride that all three of his daughters received the same standard of education as his three sons.' He smiled with a glimmer of pride of his own. 'He and my mother saw to it that all six of us went to university and then on to pursue independent careers. I have one sister who's a lawyer and another who's a chemist.'

Giselle was quietly astounded. 'I'm impressed,' she murmured, then added quickly, deliberately negating the spontaneous compliment, 'But then, I suppose, for people like your family access to such privileges is that much easier.'

Fayiz paused, his eyes still on her, and drank his brandy thoughtfully. 'Explain, *habibiti*, what you mean by that.'

Giselle laughed inwardly. What a display of innocence! He knew exactly what she meant! 'I mean——' she toyed with the stem of her glass, honing the sharp, cutting edge of her voice '—that life for the rich is invariably easier. The poor can't always send their daughters to university, however enlightened they may happen to be.' She paused and fixed the unblinking black eyes. 'But then someone like yourself isn't likely to know about such nasty, squalid things as poverty.'

'You think not?'

'How could you?'

'I might surprise you.'

She held his eyes. 'I doubt that very much.'

He shook his head and laid his glass down, a strange smile quirking at the corners of his lips. 'In that case you may find it difficult to believe that when I arrived in England fifteen years ago to study at the London School of Economics, I didn't have two pennies to my name. I lived in a bedsit in Fulham Park Road and worked nights as a bartender in a pub in Piccadilly.'

'*You*?' He was spinning some elaborate hoax, but she didn't believe it for a minute. 'And what about the generous allowance that your father no doubt sent you? Did you fritter it all away on gambling and loose women?'

One dark eyebrow lifted. His smile had faded. 'There was no gambling nor any loose women to speak of—and, alas, most assuredly no allowance.'

He wasn't joking. She could sense he spoke the truth. 'How come? Had you fallen out with your father?'

'No, I never did that, I'm thankful to say. But the provision of an allowance for any of his children was something well beyond his means.' As he paused, a bitter smile touched his lips. 'My parents were the children of Armenian refugees who had fled to the Lebanon in 1915, a bitter date in our people's history. They settled in Beirut and, like many of their kind, were desperately poor for many years.'

He sighed. 'But, gradually, by dint of hard work their situation began to improve and my parents did reasonably well for a while. They ran a little grocery store and saved every single penny they could. Of course everything changed when the civil war started. Like that of thousands of others, their living was ruined. By the time they were both blown up by a car bomb—along with one of my brothers and my eldest sister—their business was completely on its knees. But one consolation was that they lived just long enough to see one of their dearest dreams fulfilled. Just a matter of weeks before the tragedy my youngest sister had been the last of us to graduate.'

There was a silence, brief and thunderous, as he concluded his story, then Giselle leaned towards him, her cheeks taut and pale. 'Oh, Fayiz, I had no idea! I assumed you'd always had an easy life and that you'd always lived like this. How stupid of me!

I never suspected——' Her words filled the room
in a gush of shame. Of the two of them she was the
one who had been privileged in the safe,
untroubled life she had led. He, by contrast, had
known suffering and deprivation far beyond the
bounds of most people's imagining. She broke off
helplessly and stared across at him, her eyes
silently begging his forgiveness.

Without a flicker of hesitation it was granted. His
gaze was steady. 'How could you have known?
None of us finds it particularly easy to look beyond
the obvious evidence of our eyes.'

She threw him a look of heartfelt gratitude and
observed with a note of wonder in her voice, 'So
all of this——' she looked around her '——you've
managed to achieve all on your own?'

'Yes, I'm afraid so—with some help from the
gods.' He smiled a smile that was faintly apologetic
as he went on to explain, 'After a childhood spent
teetering on the edge of poverty, with death and
destruction all around, I was determined that I
would never be hungry, or at the mercy of others,
ever again. And even more importantly——' he
held her eyes, his expression uncompromising and
hard '——that my children would never even
remotely know the destruction of the soul that such
insecurity brings.'

The fine black eyes blazed with emotion and,
just for a moment, Giselle felt that emotion reach
out like a strong hand and touch her heart. Just for
a moment, she saw before her the splendour and
the courage of the man behind the mask. Fayiz was

not what she had thought he was, no hard, uncaring monster—as she had realised the first moment she had seen him with Rasha. Though there was still, she sensed, much that remained hidden. What she had been privileged to see today was but a brief, fleeting glimpse into a tightly locked soul.

But at least now she understood his attachment to his daughter. 'You must miss Rasha,' she observed with sudden compassion, 'seeing her so seldom as you do.'

He let out a sigh that seemed to shudder to his soul, then reached for his glass and, in one gulp, drained it. 'One weekend in four is all I have with her, and that is the cruellest sacrifice I have ever had to make. At the time of the divorce I made the mistake of allowing my ex-wife uncontested custody. I foolishly thought it would be in Rasha's best interests that she be brought up by her mother.' He sighed again, harshly, and laid the glass down. 'Now I regret that decision more than anything.'

At the shaft of raw pain that darkened his eyes Giselle felt the warmth of compassion rise within her. For a moment then he had looked so vulnerable, and she longed to reach out and reassure him.

But she dared not offer her hand to him for fear of inviting his harsh rejection. He would welcome sympathy from no man, she sensed, and, most assuredly, from no woman.

Quietly, to comfort him, she murmured, 'I'm sure you did right to leave Rasha with her mother. Small children, and especially little girls, need the presence of a mother.'

He smiled a hard smile. 'And most courts would agree with you. Indeed so would I in general terms. But the suitability of the mother must also be considered—and, in this particular case, that suitability is questionable.'

'Why do you say that?' He had made her curious.

'Because my ex-wife is a bitch, a greedy, selfish bitch, with all the vicious guile of the worst sort of female! But then that is something I ought to have known after seven years of marriage to her!'

The unexpected vehemence of his answer was shocking. Giselle's senses jolted beneath its ferocity. She looked across at him, eyes dark with disapproval. This was more like the Fayiz she was familiar with—full of angry vitriol and mean contempt for the female of the species.

And the evening was spoiled. She felt nothing but relief as he rose abruptly to his feet and told her,

'We've talked enough. I think it's time for bed.'

Giselle rose without a word as he picked up his jacket and slung it casually over his shoulder. Then, as he swung round and started to head for the door, she followed, her eyes on the back of his neck.

She had known what he was. She had known it from the start. He was an arrogant, intolerant, hateful chauvinist.

So why, as she followed him out into the hall, did she suddenly feel quite overwhelmed by a deep, illogical sense of betrayal and an angry, numbing disappointment?

CHAPTER SEVEN

'I THINK we ought to go riding this afternoon and keep the beach and the fun-fair till tomorrow.'

Rasha curled her nose at her father's suggestion. 'I want to go to the beach today,' she insisted.

'But you told me you wanted to ride on Candy. Harry's been getting her ready especially for you coming. We really ought to go down to the stables today.'

'We can pass by the stables on the way to the seaside, just to say hello,' Rasha offered—and at her blatant wiliness Fayiz roared with laughter and reached out to tousle her hair with his hand. He turned to Giselle with a helpless gesture.

'What can I possibly do with a little monkey like this?'

Giselle smiled back at him and shrugged amusedly. 'I wouldn't know. She's much too clever for me.'

It was Saturday morning and they were having a leisurely late breakfast out on the patio together. Somewhat to her surprise Fayiz had insisted that, far from intending to banish her to the kitchen, he wanted her to spend as much time as possible with him and Rasha.

'This weekend's to be a holiday for you as well. You deserve it. Just so long as you don't mind giving Mrs Pennygreen a hand when she needs it.'

And although the weekend had scarcely started it was already turning out to be quite a revelation. In spite of that unfortunate hiccup of last night on the subject of his ex-wife and women in general, Giselle was aware that she was seeing Fayiz as she could never in her wildest dreams have imagined him. And she both liked and approved of this new side she was seeing.

In the company of his daughter he assumed a new persona—relaxed and funny and quite without hard edges. Last night when he had told her about his background he had allowed her a brief glimpse into his soul. Now he seemed to be showing her he had a heart as well.

And, what was more, a soft heart—at least for his daughter, who was still refusing to go along with his plans.

'But, Papa, if we go riding today, it might rain tomorrow and then we couldn't go swimming. If we go swimming today, it would be much better. We can still go horse riding in the rain.'

As Fayiz shook his head at the childish logic and sat back, smiling, in his seat, Giselle had the definite impression that this good-natured wrangle might go on for some time.

'While you two are battling it out,' she interceded, 'I think I'll take a quick trip to Honeybee Cottage.' She met Fayiz's eyes as he glanced round to look at her. 'I thought I'd take advantage of being in the area to check that everything's all right.'

'Good idea,' Fayiz agreed. 'Take the

Mercedes—the one you used before. You'll find the keys are in the kitchen. Mrs Pennygreen will show you where.' He smiled across at his bright-eyed daughter. 'Rasha and I will amuse ourselves until you get back.'

Giselle's visit to the cottage was brief and satisfactory. The graduate girl student to whom she had sub-let it had kept it in immaculate order. But the girl had guests, so Giselle didn't linger, just picked up a few bits of extra clothing, said her goodbyes and headed back to the car.

As she climbed in and started up the engine, she glanced at the little whitewashed cottage with its pretty bow windows and roses round the door and felt a curious sensation—a strange detachment, almost a glimmer of regret—to think that in just a couple of months' time, when her assignment in Belgravia was over, she herself would be installed in the cottage once again.

Surprised at her feelings, she chastised herself. She should be celebrating, not regretting! Personal and professional independence, after all, were what awaited her at the end of her London stint. How could it be possible, now that they were so nearly hers, that the thought of these two cherished prizes failed quite singularly to ignite even the faintest trace of triumph in her heart?

Was it, perhaps, that she had grown so used to the sumptuous luxury of Belgravia that she regretted the prospect of giving it up? Had she grown soft, she wondered, in the past few weeks? Or greedy, perhaps?

But the reason, she knew, was none of these. It was, quite simply and indisputably, that she realised how much she was going to miss Fayiz.

The admission faintly chilled her, for she could not deny it. As impossible as he was, as much as he infuriated her, he would leave a vast, empty gap in her life. As no other human being she had ever known before, he aroused her and stimulated her and made her feel alive. Without the colourful presence of Fayiz, she feared, life was going to be very dull indeed.

Back at Chiltham Hall Giselle parked the Mercedes and, following the happy squeals of childish laughter, headed round to the back of the house. And there, in a flat, secluded corner of the garden, she could see that some croquet hoops had been set out. She paused before either of the players caught sight of her and, hidden by some trees, watched the scene before her.

Father and daughter laughing together, thoroughly enjoying themselves. Fayiz, in casual blue cotton trousers and a matching open-necked blue cotton shirt, looking heart-stoppingly handsome and totally carefree, as he helped Rasha wield her mini-mallet. And the little girl, in her tomboy's dungarees, following his every movement with wide, adoring eyes.

Yes, there was no denying she would miss him—she would even, ridiculously, miss his little daughter. She felt a pang of regret tighten sharply round her heart—and chastised herself brusquely. She was just being foolish. Then, with a determined shrug, she stepped out of the trees and, forcing a bright smile, headed towards them.

'Hi there, you two!' she called out. 'Which one of you is winning?'

Two laughing faces turned towards her. 'This little demon,' Fayiz confirmed. 'She's such an expert she's beating me hollow.'

'But you nearly won the last game,' Rasha quickly pointed out, making her father's smile grow even wider, as he reached down to stroke her hair with his hand.

'Now, let's see how good Giselle is.' He took a spare mallet from the edge of the lawn and handed it to the Titian-haired girl. 'Come on, we'll have another game with the three of us against each other.'

Giselle took the mallet and made a face. 'Perhaps I should just watch,' she suggested. 'I've never played croquet before.'

But Rasha scoffed at her reluctance. 'It's easy!' she insisted.

And Fayiz pointed out, holding her eyes, 'Don't worry, there's a first time for everything. Rasha and I will teach you.'

And they taught her well, for she won the first game, though she had a definite suspicion it was a fix. In the course of the game, more than one conspiratorial glance had passed surreptitiously between father and daughter. Then at the end of it, as honours were bestowed, Fayiz solemnly sought Rasha's approval as he declared, 'I think Giselle did very well. I think she ought to be admitted to the club.'

And, equally solemnly, Rasha agreed. 'I think so too, Papa,' she nodded.

'What club?' Giselle frowned as Rasha explained,

'Our private club, Papa's and mine. Only special people are allowed to join.'

'In that case, I'm honoured,' Giselle assured her. And, indeed, she genuinely could not have felt more honoured if she had just been granted membership of the most exclusive and prestigious club in the land!

For, like her father, Giselle could tell that, in spite of her outward, easy-going charm, Rasha had the kind of careful temperament that demands proof of worth before offering friendship. It was definitely not some cut-price commodity to be handed out routinely to just anyone!

So she felt doubly honoured when, later that afternoon, quite unexpectedly, Fayiz confirmed, 'You've made quite a hit with Rasha, you know. It's not everyone she takes to the way she's taken to you.'

'She's made a hit with me as well. I think she's a super little girl.'

They were down on the beach, stretched out on the sand, Rasha having won with points to spare that earlier confrontation with her father. And so far the victor had been the only one brave enough to defy the moderate English summer temperatures and change into a swimming costume. She was down at the water's edge, making sand pies, while the two grown-ups, in jeans and T-shirts, watched her progress from a few yards off.

'She was asking me earlier if it would be possible for you to come and share our next weekend with us?' Despite the smile in his voice, his eyes were serious. He seemed to be waiting for her answer.

'That would be lovely—if I'm not intruding.' For some reason she was not sure of Giselle glanced away.

'There's no question of intruding.'

'Then I'd love to. I've thoroughly enjoyed myself today.'

It was absolutely true, she reflected to herself. She'd relished every single minute of it. Down here on the beach and, earlier, at the fun-fair, where they had eaten candy-floss and gone for a ride in the bumper cars, the three of them had seemed to fit together quite naturally, like one happy little family, amid all the dozens of others. It was an experience she wouldn't mind repeating in the slightest.

She glanced across at Fayiz beneath her lashes as he turned for a moment to check up on Rasha. If only he were always this easy to get on with she would have absolutely no complaints at all!

They got back to Chiltham Hall just after five-thirty. Time for Rasha to have her bath and supper, plus a bedtime story from her father, before finally being tucked up at seven-thirty.

Giselle was in the kitchen, about to prepare dinner, when Fayiz appeared in the kitchen doorway. 'Forget about cooking this evening,' he told her. 'You and I are going out for a meal.'

She laid down the onion she'd just started peeling and raised her eyes in surprise to look at him. 'Out?' she echoed a trifle foolishly. 'You mean out to a restaurant?'

'That's precisely what I mean. I've booked us a table at Emilio's,' he grinned, naming the very best restaurant in the area. 'Our reservation's for eight-thirty, so you'd better hurry up and start getting ready.'

'But what about Rasha?' Giselle stared in confusion. Emilio's? A reservation? What had come over him? 'We can't just go off and leave her alone here.'

'I've thought of that, and I've phoned Mrs Pennygreen. She's coming over to babysit in half an hour's time.' Then, as she continued to stand there in total bemusement, he came striding across to her, took the half-peeled onion and dropped it casually into the bin. The black eyes met hers with a good-humoured twinkle. 'Now go off and get changed. And wear something pretty!' Up in her bedroom Giselle stared at her wardrobe. Wear something pretty! The nerve of the man! Even when issuing an invitation to dinner, he couldn't resist throwing in an order!

Yet, all the same, through her mild irritation, a fountain of excitement was bubbling up inside her. It was such ages since anyone had taken her to dinner. She hadn't had a night out like this since Ken—and that had been so long ago she could scarcely remember it!

She glanced critically at the modest row of dresses, suddenly grateful for her trip to the cottage this morning. There was nothing here that even remotely approached the standard of attire Fayiz was used to in his companions, but at least now she had a couple of dresses to choose from instead of just one or two summer skirts and tops.

Emilio's, she repeated to herself, frowning slightly. She had never been there, but she knew its reputation. An evening out in such a classy establishment definitely demanded the best.

And her best, she decided, was a simple shift, kingfisher blue, with a wide tan belt, a dramatic contrast to her bright hair, and worn with a pair of high-heeled tan sandals. She brushed her tawny mane into place, adjusted her make-up and sprayed on some scent, then paused to regard her reflection critically.

What on earth was she getting so excited about? This evening, to Fayiz, meant nothing special. He was probably just bored with domesticity, fancied dining out at a restaurant for a change and had felt obliged to invite her along.

She leaned forward to meet her eyes in the mirror, suddenly quite appalled at their sparkling brightness. And all this is to you, my girl, she warned, is a routine evening with your employer! Absolutely nothing to get so wound up about!

Yet as she hurried downstairs to join him in the drawing-room and he rose politely from his chair, in spite of herself, Giselle's heart missed a beat. In the immaculate dark suit, white shirt and blue tie the devil himself could not have looked more handsome. And though she knew she should be well used to his looks by now, their impact on her senses never ceased to astound her.

He proceeded to astound her even further as he took a step towards her and kissed her cheek. 'Allow me. I bought you this.' From nowhere he produced a small plastic box, undid the ribbon that held it shut and, very carefully, lifted the lid. He smiled at her. 'I must be psychic! It's a perfect contrast to your dress.' Then, leaning towards her, so that she burned, he pinned the delicate pink orchid to her dress.

Alarm bells were ringing in Giselle's head. So this evening was not spontaneous, after all. Quite clearly, she could see now, it must have been planned—unless of course Fayiz kept a supply of orchids conveniently to hand!

As he bent towards her, she could feel his warmth and the intimate whisper of his breath on her face, and the hands that barely touched her, yet seemed to consume her, were sending electric shockwaves through her veins.

But get a grip on yourself! the voice of reason warned her, as she felt herself inwardly melt at his nearness. Don't be taken in by this clever seduction! For you can bet your life, as sure as cats have claws, this clever, manipulative man is up to something!

As they made their way down the stone steps to the car, Giselle was watching him from the corner of her eye. He's trying to soften me up, she thought suspiciously, trying to get round me for some reason. In fact, it suddenly struck her, this entire weekend, most probably, had been part of some devious plan. She felt a flash of inward anger at her earlier naïve excitement and at the way he had so adroitly taken her in. This entire exhibition of chivalry and charm was undoubtedly nothing but a sham.

As with a courteous helping hand he assisted her into the passenger seat, she was more than ever convinced that she was right. Perhaps it was that dreaded dinner party for fifty that she had joked about so often with Ella. Or maybe he had something even more sinister neatly concealed up his immaculately tailored sleeve.

As she sat back in her seat, her backbone turned to iron. Let him do his worst, she told herself determinedly. Let him play his little game, and she would play along with it. Then when he finally put his cards on the table, whatever his request might prove to be, she would respond with a resounding and implacable negative! Just for once he would be the one left with egg on his face!

The restaurant was already busy as the waiter showed them to their table, and Giselle was aware of the nods and smiles from several of the other diners that accompanied Fayiz across the room. He was evidently no stranger to this watering hole of the local gentry.

Warming to the game ahead, Giselle glanced across the table at her handsome companion and looked boldly into the jet-black eyes. 'You come here a lot, do you?' she enquired pleasantly. 'Everybody seems to know you.'

'It's a first-class place. The food is excellent.' He paused to bestow a heart-stopping smile. 'Almost up to the standard of your own culinary skills.'

Oh, yes, he was definitely up to something, she confirmed to herself as her heartbeat resumed. All this unsolicited praise and deference were not like him at all!

'Flatterer!' she responded, playing her part, letting her lashes flutter coyly to her cheeks. Let him believe that he had her in the palm of his hand—then, when he least expected it, she would snap off his fingers!

As the waiter arrived to take their orders, Giselle allowed herself to be guided through the menu by Fayiz. 'The asparagus is excellent,' he advised. 'Or maybe you would prefer some pasta?'

She smiled demurely. 'Asparagus for me. If I don't watch my figure, nobody else will.'

'But your figure is perfect. You have no worries on that score. Go on, let yourself go just this once!'

She feigned reluctance. 'I shouldn't really——'

'I'm going to have it. Come on, let me tempt you.'

Giselle took a deep breath, feigning indecision, then shrugged her capitulation with a fluttering smile. 'OK, you win.' She giggled to herself. He would soon discover how far that was from the truth!

In the meantime, he was keeping up the charm, and it flowed as effortlessly from him as honey from a honeycomb. And in spite of her determination to resist him, Giselle was all too uncomfortably conscious that in this new, seductive mould Fayiz was dangerously beguiling.

It was no effort to keep up her sham flirtation. In fact, she was barely aware of pretending. His jokes, after all, were genuinely funny. She didn't need to force a laugh. And when he reached across the table to touch her hand softly the rush of colour to her cheeks that reflected the sudden warm rush in her heart would have been very hard to fake.

It was truly a great pity, she found herself thinking, that this cynical performance was merely an act.

'How was the pasta? Did I do right to tempt you?'

Giselle laid down her fork. 'It was very good.' And as she looked into his eyes, those velvet-black eyes that were gazing unblinkingly back into hers, she had to steel herself not to fall under their spell. Keep your wits about you, the voice of resistance exhorted her. This man is a master of manipulation. If you start to soften, before you realise what's happening he'll have you skinned and hung up to dry!

The waiter came and took their plates away. Fayiz smiled across at her. 'Now let's hope you enjoy the veal.'

'I'm sure I shall.' She smiled back at him coquettishly, but with a sudden anxious stab at the way her pulse rate had reacted to the dark, mysterious look in his eyes. Concentrate, concentrate! the voice commanded. Remember, the whole thing's nothing but a scam!

The veal was even more delicious than the pasta and the wine that accompanied it was a treat to the palate. And the redoubtable Fayiz, if such a thing were possible, grew more irresistibly charming with every passing minute.

'Tell me about yourself, Giselle,' he insisted, carefully laying his wine glass aside. 'Tell me about your family. Have you brothers and sisters?'

This was a particularly clever and subtle tactic, pretending to be interested in her background, and Giselle had to struggle to remain aloof, as she responded in as little detail as possible.

'I have a sister—her name's Annette. She's a couple of years older than me.'

'Is she married?'

'Yes—to Jim. He's a decorator. He runs his own business in Colchester.'

'And your parents—are they still alive?'

'Very much so. They live up in Hereford.'

Fayiz smiled understandingly. 'It must be a little sad for them that both of their daughters live so far away.'

He was right. Giselle nodded. 'Yes, they were disappointed when I decided to follow in Annette's footsteps and moved to the other side of the country as well. I think they'd hoped that at least one of us would stay. But they're the kind of parents,' she added proudly, 'who are happy just so long as their children are.'

'That's the best kind to have,' Fayiz agreed, smiling. Then he added on a slightly more serious note, 'I hope it's the type of parent I'll always be to Rasha. I hope I'll always put her interests before my own.'

'I'm sure you will,' Giselle responded instantly. 'You seem to me a most conscientious and caring father.' She stopped short, deeply irritated at herself for this generous and totally spontaneous appraisal. In spite of all her efforts, he had made her so relaxed that she was in serious danger of being won round by his charm.

The trouble was he was almost impossible to resist, Giselle acknowledged bitterly to herself, as their meat plates at last were carried away and the waiter brought them dishes of delicious zabaglione. Whatever it is he wants of me, she thought, he must want it very badly indeed to subject me to this overpowering seduction routine!

But somehow she managed to stay in control, though outwardly, she knew, she must appear quite bowled over. She was feeling quite proud of herself as their dessert dishes were removed and the delicate porcelain coffee-cups brought. Surely this was the point at which Fayiz would reveal the purpose of the evening? The point at which she would finally have the pleasure of putting him firmly in his place!

And she was right. For once, he acted predictably.

As the waiter poured their coffee and left them alone, Fayiz leaned across the table towards her, an unfathomable expression on his face. 'I expect you were wondering why I brought you here this evening. Well, I do have a reason. There's something I want to ask you.'

Giselle felt a rush of malicious anticipation. Prepare for deflation, she thought, smiling back at him. 'Oh, really?' she enquired pleasantly, touching her coffee-spoon. 'Ask away. I'm listening.'

He took a deep breath and paused for a moment, his eyes intent as they swept over her face. 'This may take you a little by surprise,' he told her, igniting in her the inward flicker of a smile. At this point nothing in the world could surprise her! And she had her answer prepared, whatever his demand!

But she almost fell stone dead from her chair as he reached for her hand and went on to tell her,

'What I want to ask you is—will you marry me?'

CHAPTER EIGHT

'I BEG your pardon?' Giselle gaped at him blankly. So much for the predictability she had inwardly accused him of! She was the one now who felt totally deflated. 'Would you mind saying that again?' she stuttered.

Fayiz's dark eyes never flickered. They held hers steadily as he repeated, 'I asked you, Giselle, if you would marry me.'

That was precisely what she'd thought he'd said, but even with the benefit of a second hearing it made absolutely no sense at all. 'You're joking, of course?' She smiled a watery smile, reflecting how neatly he had turned the tables on her. She had been the one planning to pull the rug out from under him, and instead, that was precisely what he had done to her!

Her heart fluttering, her head spinning, she peered across the table at him. 'You *are* joking, aren't you?' she insisted.

'Why should I be joking?' He leaned towards her. 'Is it really such a preposterous suggestion to make?'

'Yes, as a matter of fact it is!' Giselle blinked at him in open astonishment. 'Why on earth would I want to marry you? Or you me, for that matter!'

Fayiz leaned back a little in his chair and seemed to study her carefully before answering, absorbing every minute detail of her features with that disconcerting ebony gaze. He laced his long, copper-coloured fingers casually across his chest and frowned as though assessing a desirable piece of merchandise. 'I can answer the second part of that question quite easily. I believe you would make me a most suitable wife.'

'Suitable?' The word had a calculating ring. 'In what way suitable? Kindly explain.'

'In all ways.' He raised one dark eyebrow and elaborated, 'I have been watching you closely over the past few weeks and I have been most impressed with what I have seen. You are a personable and highly intelligent young lady who knows how to conduct herself in all sorts of company. You are modest in your behaviour, and refined—the sort of partner one would never have to fear might cause one some kind of social embarrassment.'

'One wouldn't want that!' Giselle smiled sarcastically, struggling to fight back the wave of indignation that was building up inside her like steam inside a pressure cooker. And though she was tempted to cut the confrontation short and tell him, quite bluntly, what to do with his offer, some perverse, morbid instinct prompted her to ask,

'And what other attributes do you deem to qualify me for such an elevated position?' Since she was being summed up and evaluated so dispassionately, like some piece of horseflesh at an auction, she might as well hear the whole assessment. This, after all, was an entirely new experience.

By the thin smile that flickered across his lips Giselle could tell that her sarcasm was not lost on him. But it appeared to have no more effect on him than a bubble bursting in the wind. He continued to regard her over his loosely laced fingers, the dark eyes unrepentant as he told her, 'You are an excellent hostess and a first-class cook, both high on the list of attributes I seek. And I think you would make a good mother for Rasha. The two of you get on extremely well.'

In a flash Giselle was certain she understood all—the entire devious purpose behind this weekend. She had been brought to Chiltham Hall specifically to meet Rasha, in order that he might judge her suitability as a stepmother. As he had told her, she had apparently passed all his other tests. This one with his daughter had been the last one remaining.

With a clench of distaste for his computer-like coldbloodedness, tight-lipped, Giselle glared across the table at him. 'I see. I seem to fit the bill pretty well.' The gold of her eyes had darkened with anger. 'Do you have anything else to add to your list?'

Fayiz unlaced his fingers and leaned towards her, resting his elbows on the table. A more intimate, faintly amused expression had crept now into the steady dark eyes. A strange smile softened the lines of his mouth.

'Oh, yes, *habibiti*, there is one more thing, an irresistible bonus in the circumstances.' He let his gaze glide over her before continuing, bringing a touch of warmth to her fury-frozen cheeks, as he caressed with his eyes the soft swell of her breasts. 'You and I share a mutual physical attraction, such an essential ingredient in any marriage. One thing, at least, we could always be sure of—the sexual side of our union would be most fulfilling.'

The warmth of faint embarrassment that coloured Giselle's cheeks had escalated to a blaze of fury. Literally speechless with anger, she glowered across the table at him. How dared he have the unutterable impertinence to come out and say such a thing to her face?

Fayiz raised one coal-black eyebrow. 'Do you deny it?' he challenged boldly. 'Surely you would not be so false?'

He was right about that. There could be no gainsaying the animal attraction that existed between them. Even now, through the steam heat of her anger, just the thought of his warm touch on her flesh was sending darts of erotic, secret pleasure skittering unstoppably over her flesh.

But that aspect of her feelings for him was but a regrettable anomaly, and one, alas, that she appeared unable to control. It angered her that he should hold it up in front of her. It was crude and tasteless of him in the extreme. She narrowed her eyes and told him so. 'I'm afraid I find it insulting in the extreme that you should choose to debase the conversation by alluding unnecessarily to such things!'

The dark brows shot up again. He looked deep into her face. 'Debase, *habibiti*?' he enquired with wry amusement. 'What is so debasing about the subject of sex?'

Giselle hated him for his cool composure and for his ability to wrong-foot her at every turn. 'I find nothing debasing about the subject of sex,' she assured him, holding the dark eyes uneasily. 'What I find debasing is the context into which you introduced it.'

'The context of marriage?' He regarded her mockingly. 'Surely marriage is its right and most proper context?'

He was running her round in circles, making her look stupid. She flashed at him resentfully, 'That's not what I meant!'

'So what did you mean?' He paused for a moment, then widened his eyes in mock-illumination. 'Ah! I know what you meant! You disapprove of sex not in the context of marriage, but in the context of a marriage *proposal*! Am I not right, *jamila* Giselle? That is what you found so debasing.' Then, before she could answer, he added disparagingly, 'Would you rather I had used the word "love" instead?'

Giselle glared back at him disapprovingly. Trust him to disparage the concept of love! 'In my book love is an essential ingredient when it comes to considerations of marriage!'

'So you're a romantic, are you, sweet Giselle?' His tone was taunting, almost harsh. 'Take it from one who has bitter experience that love is far from being all it's cracked up to be.'

She tossed him a hard look. 'How would you

know? I doubt you've ever loved a woman in your life!'

A flash of some dark emotion glittered in his eyes—bright and vivid, acutely vulnerable, reminding her briefly of the previous evening when he had revealed so much about himself. But, almost before she had a chance to absorb it, it had been doused and replaced by a look of black arrogance. 'Love is for fools—surely you know that? I seem to remember you have some experience yourself.'

Giselle blinked for a moment. He was referring to Ken. Fickle, faithless, half-forgotten Ken. 'That wasn't really love. I only thought it was. Love doesn't flicker and die overnight.'

He laughed without humour, a harsh, dismissive sound, though the dark eyes seemed watchful as they burned into hers, almost as though her plain words of wisdom had struck some unexpected chord. Then he looked away with a gesture of impatience and sat back a little in his seat. 'All this foolish talk of love has diverted us.' Then his eyes swung back to hers again. 'I'm still waiting for your answer.'

'My answer?' Giselle gave a glimmer of a smile. 'I would have thought my answer was perfectly obvious. I would never for one moment consider marrying you.'

'Never?' He seemed unperturbed by her answer. 'You must consider the advantages before rushing to such a judgement.' He lifted his napkin from his lap and tossed it casually on to the table, then turned briefly to catch the attention of the waiter.

'Bring the bill, please,' he commanded brusquely.

He turned back to Giselle. 'Just think, *habibiti*,' he purred in a soft voice, watching her closely. 'That easy life that you so long for would be yours at last.'

'And what would be easy about being married to you? I can think of few things that appeal to me less.'

'Keep thinking, *habibiti*,' he advised with a smile. 'After a bit of serious contemplation, you may well feel inclined to change your mind.' As the waiter brought the bill to him, he extracted a note from his wallet and tossed it casually on to the plate. 'I can offer you security and an enviable lifestyle—plus the pleasure, of course, of being my consort. Think well before giving me your final answer. You are unlikely ever to receive a better offer.'

He had already received her final answer, but he was too damned arrogant to believe it. As the waiter moved off, Giselle grasped the opportunity to put him firmly in his place. 'Your ex-wife evidently didn't find that marriage to you was such an irresistible pleasure.' She regarded him nastily. 'Why should I be different?'

He did not flinch. He merely smiled at her with a look of total, unshakeable composure. 'Believe me, if I thought that you were no different from that woman, I would never for one minute have considered making you such a proposal.' He held her eyes in a dark embrace. 'Think well, *habibiti*. I'm prepared to give you time.'

He could give her till Doomsday and it would make no difference. There wasn't really a single thing to think about. Yet, in the taxi home, she enquired curiously, as a sudden question slipped into her head, 'Why did you say that I would make a good mother for Rasha? Even if I were mad enough to consider your proposal, my suitability as a stepmother is scarcely of prime importance, considering that Rasha lives with her real mother.'

He smiled obscurely without meeting her eyes. 'She lives with her real mother for the moment. But the beauty of life is that it constantly changes.'

'You mean you're hoping to gain custody of Rasha yourself?'

This time, as he answered, he did meet her eyes, every line in his face echoing the resolve in his words. 'I'm not just hoping, it's my firm intention. I shall see to it that that child is returned to me if it's the very last thing I ever do!'

So that was what was behind his offer, Giselle decided later as she got ready for bed. He had resolved to fight his ex-wife for custody of Rasha and having a new wife in the wings would undoubtedly help his cause.

Hadn't he admitted to her himself that the courts, as a rule, tend not to look too favourably on single fathers as custodians of small daughters? In his usual calculating way, he had thought up a scheme to put that right.

Up in the welcome seclusion of her room Giselle's hands were trembling as she pulled on her nightdress. The more she thought about it, the more angry she became. And not just angry, hurt as well that he should have the barefaced gall to try to recruit her as a convenient housekeeper and mother to his daughter.

And to think that just a matter of hours ago she had been on the point of seriously revising her opinion of him!

She snatched back the bedclothes and climbed between them, slamming her head angrily against the pillows and glowering furiously into space. His ex-wife, doubtless, had been treated likewise and that was why she had upped and left. And now he was planning to take Rasha away from her, no doubt out of some kind of personal spite. Though no one could deny that he loved the child dearly, presumably her mother loved her too. It would be nothing less than an act of criminality if his vicious little plan were to succeed.

Well, he definitely won't have me as an ally, Giselle thought with some bitterness as she turned out the light. How right she had been in her initial assessment of him! Sex objects and servants, that was all women were to him. If she were to join forces with anyone in the coming battle over Rasha, it would not be with him but with his ex-wife!

The week that followed their return to London was extra busy, to Giselle's great relief, and the subject of Fayiz's marriage proposal, to her even greater relief, was not raised again.

Not that it had been forgotten. She was aware of

that. From time to time, as she went about her business, she was aware of him following her with dark watchful eyes—almost as though, like some latter-day Svengali, he was seeking to bend her to his will.

But, even without trying, she knew she could resist him. No power existed—not on earth, nor in heaven—that could persuade her to enter into a marriage of convenience.

Yet in spite of her strength of self-possession, her unbending certainty in where she stood, an irrational sense of deep despondency had settled upon her like a shroud. There was no pleasure any more in the daily round that had previously so fascinated and entertained her. She felt dull and weighted with a sense of drudgery. Everything she did felt like a chore.

She had tried, dispassionately, to analyse this change in her. Why had the sparkle gone from her life? Nothing fundamental, after all, had altered, so why this sudden terrible sense of hopelessness?

It had begun, inexorably, to descend on her the very next day after Fayiz's proposal. As her anger had lifted, the gloom had replaced it, filling the dark, empty place in her heart. And, however hard she fought to dispel it, it continued to cling like a dull, heavy weight.

It was a foolish reaction, she chided herself tirelessly. Her initial burst of anger had been more appropriate. Why should it matter that he had insulted her with that cold, calculated proposal of marriage? Wasn't it simply one more example of the heartless automaton that he really was?

Just a few short weeks ago she would have accepted that argument. But now, alas, she knew very different. Fayiz was far from being the heartless automaton that he somehow chose to present to the world. He was capable of love—deep, selfless love—she had seen it glowing from his face. And she had caught, more than once, a glimpse of the vulnerability that lay hidden behind the iron mask.

She sighed at the thought. Be it foolish or not, she had developed an affection, along with a deep respect and admiration, for the Fayiz she knew lurked behind the façade. He was a man in a million, brave and special. The sort of a man a woman could easily fall in love with. And that was why it hurt so much that he had treated her with such a show of contempt.

A marriage of convenience, that was what he had offered, with the 'irresistible bonus' of good sex thrown in. And though he had been right about their mutual attraction—the way he made her flesh burn was beyond denying—as she had told him then, although he had mocked her, she required a great deal more from marriage than that.

She allowed her mind to drift in sympathy to his ex-wife, whom, no doubt, he had likewise treated with humiliating disdain. No wonder she had been driven to leave him. What woman could endure to be so shabbily treated?

It is as well, she decided, that I have kept hold of my own heart. At least he can do me no serious harm. Yet she was counting the days to the end of her contract. The sooner her time in Belgravia was over, the safer she would begin to feel.

It was ten days precisely after that weekend in the country, just as her black mood seemed at its blackest, that events took a sudden and remarkable turn.

It was one of Fayiz's dinner party nights and Giselle was in the kitchen, beavering away in the preparation of a particularly tricky rice dish, when all at once the doorbell rang.

She laid down her mixing spoon and wiped her hands on her apron, muttering a heartfelt 'Damn!' as she glanced at her watch. Who on earth could it be at this hour? she wondered. It was only just gone seven and Fayiz's guests were not expected till after eight.

Well, there was only one way to find out, she decided, as, impatiently, the doorbell rang again. With a toss of her head she shook back her hair, then untied her apron and dropped it on a chair. Whoever it is, let's hope their business is brief, she prayed to herself, as she hurried out into the hall. She was just a little behind this evening and there was a mountain of vegetables still waiting to be peeled!

But as she pulled open the door, smiling politely, suddenly all thoughts of unpeeled vegetables were driven abruptly from her head.

A woman was standing on the threshold, slim and elegant and expensively dressed, and as Giselle stared at her she was suddenly conscious of an acute, almost crushing sense of unease.

'Good evening. Can I help you?' she enquired politely.

The woman looked back at her, disdain in her face. 'Good evening,' she said curtly. 'I've come to see Fayiz.'

'I'm afraid he's not here.' Giselle held her eyes, wondering why she suddenly felt so threatened. 'He should be back in about half an hour,' she offered. 'We have some very important dinner guests coming.'

'Do we indeed?' With a sneering smile the woman swept past her straight into the hall. 'In that case I'll wait for him. I'm sure he won't mind.' Then she turned in mid-stride and answered the question that Giselle, for some reason, had not dared to ask.

'I'm Gloria Davidian, by the way. Fayiz's ex-wife, to be precise.'

Giselle knew in that instant that she had known all along exactly who the woman was—though she was still uncertain as to the reason for her own illogically inhibited response. But before she could ponder further on that question she was unceremoniously spurred into action as the elegant erstwhile Mrs Davidian went sweeping through the hall and into the drawing-room, exactly as though she still owned the place.

Feeling faintly winded, Giselle followed her. There was one thing at least she had no need to ponder. Fayiz's legendary ex-wife was nothing at all as she had imagined her!

The woman paused in the middle of the room and looked around her with evident distaste at the claret décor, traditional furniture and heavy-framed oils that adorned the walls. 'So he's replaced everything, I see.' She cast a scathing glance across at Giselle. 'I suppose I shouldn't be surprised. He always did have such old-fashioned taste.'

If the barb was meant to needle Giselle, it failed miserably in its mission. She was far too busy doing some assessing herself. Curiously, her eyes swept Gloria Davidian.

She had the look of a woman who spent a great deal of time in hairdressers' and beauty parlours—not to mention at the Paris and Milan collections. She was dressed in a cream-coloured, figure-skimming dress that had French couture emblazoned all over it, and her ear-length, glossy dark brown hair appeared to have been designed by no less a craftsman.

She must once have been incredibly beautiful, Giselle could not stop herself from thinking. Her figure was perfect, her complexion dazzling and her features striking in a bold, dramatic way. The fact that, to Giselle's eyes at least, she was no longer the beauty she might have been had nothing whatsoever to do with age. Gloria, she guessed, was no more than thirty, an age at which she should be in her prime. But, tragically, her natural beauty had been marred by the hard, brittle sheen she had acquired. It showed in the unattractive set of her jaw and the icy glitter of her light brown eyes.

'So. We meet at last.' Keeping her gaze disdainfully averted, Gloria arranged herself in one of the deep red armchairs. She crossed her slim legs carefully at the ankles and laid her manicured hands along the arms. Then the brown eyes flicked up, openly hostile, as they focused on Giselle once again. 'Ever since Rasha told me about you I've been dying to have a close-up look at his tramp.'

'I beg your pardon?' Giselle blinked and glared at her, astounded by the sheer unsubtlety of the attack. 'I don't know where you got that idea from, but I can assure you you couldn't be more wrong!'

'Come, come, don't be shy. I don't blame you in the least.' Gloria smoothed the immaculate skirt of her dress and smiled a conspiratorial smile. 'As I can remember only too well, in some departments Fayiz has few equals. I'm sure you'll agree he's an excellent lover. One of a kind, in my experience. I really don't blame you in the least for climbing into bed with him.'

Why, the utter, bare-faced insolence of the woman! Giselle was suddenly consumed by a desire to knock that brittle, superior smile off her face. She took a step forward. 'If you don't mind, there are one or two things I think we should get straight——'

But that, unfortunately, was as far as she got. For in that very same instant Fayiz walked in.

The two women turned in unison to look at him, as he paused for a moment in the doorway, and it struck Giselle with a sudden cold shiver that she had never before seen such terrible anger burning in a human face.

The black brows knitted together like storm clouds and his voice was low and threatening, like thunder, as he fixed eyes like lasers on the face of his ex-wife. 'What the hell do you think you're doing here? I thought I warned you never again to set foot in this house!'

Gloria blanched beneath her salon *maquillage* as he strode across the room towards her like a tornado. Then she narrowed her eyes at him defiantly and shot back in her crisp, harsh voice, 'I suggest you listen to what I've come to tell you before you start issuing threats!'

'Do you indeed? Well, I'm listening. Kindly say your piece—*quickly*—and get out!'

As he continued to stand over her, hands on hips, fierce and magnificent in his fury, Gloria elaborately rearranged her slim legs and deliberately took her time about answering. She lowered her eyes, then raised them slowly. 'It concerns your daughter. Rasha,' she told him.

'I thought it might.' His lips quirked impatiently. 'Get on with it, then. Spit it out!'

With a look of disdain Gloria pursed her thin lips, which, clearly, she would never have dreamed of employing in anything so coarse as the act of spitting, and in measured, spiteful tones went on to inform him, 'I happen to know what you're up to, my dear. You're going to try and get your daughter back. Well, I just want you to know that you'll never succeed. I intend hanging on to that damned spoiled brat of yours! Whatever little tricks you and your slut get up to——' she cast a glance of pure vitriol in Giselle's direction before turning her blazing brown gaze once more on Fayiz '—you'll never get your hands on the child again!'

Just for a moment, a stillness descended. A terrible, terrifying, deafening stillness. Then Fayiz leaned towards her, his face awesome with anger, as though he might at any moment tear her apart.

Inwardly, Giselle applauded. That was a spectacle, she suddenly realised, she would not object to witnessing in the least.

But to her disappointment, and Gloria's relief, he restrained himself and simply growled instead, 'Get out of this house—*immediately*. You and your filthy, vicious tongue. I refuse to listen to one more word. I'm warning you, Gloria—just get out. Now!'

To her credit, Giselle conceded, Gloria recognised when she was beaten. She rose to her feet with a shrug of her slim shoulders, as though she had fully intended leaving anyway. But she couldn't resist one final salvo before turning and heading for the door. 'You really are wasting your time, you know, trying to get your hands on your beloved Rasha. I'm going to keep her from you. I'll make you suffer, you bastard! Make absolutely no mistake about that!'

Fayiz's dark eyes followed her elegant retreat. 'I've made two big mistakes in my life,' he ground after her, 'and the first and biggest was marrying you. The second was allowing you uncontested custody of our daughter at the time of our divorce. The only reason that I allowed it was to save Rasha the trauma of being used as a pawn between two warring parents. I had hoped that in time you might become a better mother, but evidently I was wrong.'

Then as Gloria paused for a moment in the doorway, eyes glittering with malice, he added ominously, 'But don't worry, I'll get my daughter back—if it's the very last thing on earth I do!'

Gloria said nothing, just threw him a look of pure poison before turning and stalking out of the room. Then the only sound in the sudden deafening silence was the sharp click of her heels receding across the hallway until the front door closed behind her with a loud, defiant slam.

Pale-faced and shaken, Giselle stared at the empty doorway, eyes fixed on the spot where the monstrous Gloria had been. Then she turned her head to glance at Fayiz, who stood there, eyes averted, his expression still like thunder. And, in spite of her furiously thudding heartbeat, she felt a smile of triumph creep round her lips.

For she was aware of a sudden bright sense of enlightenment, as though a heavy dark curtain had been drawn aside. The man who stood before her was no longer such a mystery. Suddenly, at long last, things were starting to make sense.

CHAPTER NINE

THAT evening Giselle's brain was spinning so fast she found it hard to concentrate on the dinner party. So much for the poor, downtrodden image that she had once entertained of Gloria Davidian! The woman was a witch—an evil, spiteful witch! No wonder Fayiz had reservations about women! The only thing that surprised Giselle now was that he had never actually strangled the woman!

After Gloria had gone, without a word, Fayiz had disappeared off to his room. From the incandescent look of rage on his face, he had at that point been pathologically incapable of any form of normal human communication. And Giselle hadn't blamed him in the slightest. She too had required a private moment or two in order to gather herself together.

By the time that Fayiz re-emerged, dressed in one of his immaculate black suits, Giselle had donned her waitress uniform and was beavering away busily in the kitchen. He stuck his head round the kitchen door at the very moment the doorbell rang, announcing the arrival of their guests. The dark eyes frowned, his mouth a straight line. 'Giselle, are you all right?' he asked.

She nodded at once, searching his face for signs that he too had recovered from the onslaught. A useless exercise, she thought with a smile. If they had been set upon by the hordes of Attila the Hun,

Fayiz's composure would not have deserted him. 'I'm OK, thanks.' She threw him a reassuring wink. 'There's nothing like preparing a four-course dinner for taking your mind off other things!'

He smiled sympathetically. 'Make it three courses. I'll do my best to cut things short tonight.'

In the event, he was as good as his word. It was just a few minutes after ten o'clock, as she was gratefully loading the dishwasher, that Giselle heard the familiar formal exchange of farewells from the hall.

'*A'salam u'alaikum.*'

'*Shokrun jazeelan.*'

Then, a moment later, as the front door closed, Fayiz appeared soundlessly at her side. Without a word, he took her hand and removed the lace cap from her head. 'Let's go through to the drawing-room,' he told her. 'You and I are going to have a little chat.'

He sat her down on the deep red sofa, crossed to the bar table and poured them each a drink. Then he came to sit down next to her, handing her her glass as he slipped off his jacket and tossed it carelessly on to a nearby chair. He leaned his head against the deep red damask and took a long, slow mouthful of his drink, then turned with narrowed eyes to look at her and told her in a low, earnest voice, 'I want to apologise most sincerely for that abominable scene tonight. It should never have happened and you should never have been a part of it.'

Instinctively, Giselle leaned towards him,

responding to his patent remorse. 'It wasn't your fault,' she assured him sincerely. Then she paused and added with a wry, sympathetic smile, 'Why didn't you tell me your ex-wife was a monster?'

Fayiz met her eyes and smiled in response. 'I thought I did tell you,' he argued.

Giselle found herself laughing. 'In a very restrained fashion! All you said was that she was a bitch. Not like you in the least, I may say!'

Fayiz made a face, sat back in his seat and took a mouthful of his drink. 'Would it have made any difference if I'd gone into details? Somehow I doubt it very much. I would have just sounded like a spiteful ex-husband slanging off the woman who walked out on him.'

He was probably right, she decided, watching the strong dark aquiline profile. And Fayiz, she should have known, had too much dignity to indulge in that sort of cheap behaviour. But she was curious now, more curious than ever, to know more about this ill-fated marriage of his.

Somehow knowing that he wouldn't object to the question, she leaned towards him and enquired, 'How on earth did you come to marry her? She must surely have seemed different when you first met?'

He laid his hand on her hand and, smiling, teased her, 'Curiosity killed the cat!' Then he gave her hand a good-natured squeeze. 'OK. I guess you have a right to know, especially after what happened this evening.' Then his face became serious and his eyes turned away as he began, unemotionally, to recount his story.

'We met while I was over at Harvard, doing my post-graduate degree. I was young and eager and innocent and Gloria was the beautiful, vivacious daughter of a visiting Brazilian professor.' He paused and allowed himself a bitter aside. 'She was also, as it happens, very much on the look-out for a husband who was going places—and, unfortunately, her eye fell on me.'

Fayiz shook his head and smoothed his dark hair slowly with the open palm of his hand. 'I have to admit I was a willing victim. At that time, I thought Gloria was quite a prize. It wasn't until we were actually married that I realised how wrong I'd been.'

As he paused again, Giselle could see the sudden taut lines around his jaw and mouth. This exercise in reassessing the past was evidently causing him some pain. After a moment, however, he continued,

'The trouble with Gloria, I'm afraid, is that she's greedy. She wants everything. I always knew she was ambitious—but that was all right, I am too. But what she didn't seem to realise was that in order to make money and succeed you've got to put in a hell of a lot of work and be prepared to make certain sacrifices. Especially when, like I was then, you're starting out with virtually nothing. When we came back to London and set up house, I was working for a big bank in the City—and Gloria seemed to expect that I would be working nine to five.'

He blew impatiently between his teeth and took

another swift mouthful of his drink. 'But nobody ever got to be rich by working a comfortable nine to five and spending every weekend out at parties—though Gloria adamantly refused to see that, and that was when the rows began. I was accused of neglecting her, of putting my work before our marriage—though she never seemed to have any qualms about spending the money I was earning. On the contrary, she was spending it almost as fast as I was earning it. Heaven knows how we would have managed if I *had* been earning a nine-to-five salary!

'Anyway——' he made an impatient gesture '—the whole thing was turning into a nightmare. We were actually on the point of splitting up when she became pregnant with Rasha.'

His voice, which had grown harsh, abruptly softened. 'For a short while after that, things improved a little, though she never really wanted the baby. But soon after Rasha was born the endless rows began again. The ironic thing is that, by then, I'd started to establish myself professionally and could have afforded to slacken off a little. But I began to look upon my work as a refuge from the constant domestic battlefield and I got into the habit of working late, simply to avoid going home.'

He gave a small self-mocking laugh. 'It's a habit I never got out of, I'm afraid—even after the divorce.'

'I'll vouch for that!' Giselle threw him a wry look. 'I've never known anyone who worked the hours that you do.'

'Perhaps now I do it in order to forget.' He smiled again, thoughtfully, and added, 'For the past is best forgotten, as I'm sure you'll agree. What we must concentrate on is the future.'

As his eyes held hers, their gaze deep and mysterious, Giselle felt a shiver of longing go through her. His words had sounded almost like an invitation, a veiled reiteration of his earlier proposal. And, just for a moment, it had sparked something within her—a secret desire to be a part of his future. For one skittering heartbeat she had longed for that more than she had ever longed for anything in her life.

But then the moment was gone and he was saying, 'The most pressing future I have to deal with, however, is the future of my daughter. I've already started legal proceedings to contest Gloria's right to custody—a move she has evidently already found out about—and, after this evening's little showdown, I'm more than ever determined that I shall win. The only reason Gloria wants to hang on to Rasha is in order to get at me.'

She had said as much in the course of her final outburst, Giselle remembered with distaste. In a gesture of solidarity, she commented quietly, 'Any woman who refers to her only child as "that damned spoiled brat"—and in the tone of voice that she used—is not exactly overflowing with mother love, I'd say. I think you deserve to win custody,' she added. 'At least there's no doubt at all that you love the child.'

Fayiz glanced away. 'It is not a matter of love. It

is simply a matter of what, in the end, is best for Rasha.'

For some reason Giselle found herself profoundly irked by this unexpectedly muted response. She frowned in irritation. 'Why do you do that? Why must you always hide your emotions?'

For a long, unsteady moment that seemed to stretch interminably Fayiz simply stared at her. And it was on the tip of Giselle's tongue to offer an apology. Perhaps, this time, she had gone too far. But then, to her surprise, his expression softened. He raised one black eyebrow. 'Do I?' he asked.

Giselle felt confused, unsure how to answer. Did he really want to hear the truth? But, as he continued to watch her, she took a gamble and looked him levelly in the eye. 'Yes, you do,' she told him bluntly. 'Not all the time, but most of it. You seem to want to give people the impression that you don't have any feelings at all.'

'Is that what they think?'

'I'm sure a lot of them do.'

'And you, *habibiti*? Do you think that too?'

'I have thought it at times,' she confessed quite frankly. 'But I have also caught the occasional glimpse of feeling, so I know it isn't entirely true.' She hesitated, feeling she had said enough, then asked in a low voice, 'Why do you do it?'

He was watching her closely, his eyes dark and still, as though through the mesmeric power that shone from them he was drawing her down, deep into his soul. 'Perhaps,' he said in a low, emotional voice that seemed to tremble the air about them, 'it is wise to keep one's feelings hidden when those feelings are so powerful that they threaten to overwhelm one.'

As he spoke, he had moved along the sofa towards her and now he was the merest fraction of a centimetre away. 'Do you understand what I'm saying?' he murmured.

'I think so,' Giselle nodded. 'I think I do.' She stared into his face, seeing all too clearly the burning passion that smouldered there. And though the feelings he was feeling, and making no effort to hide now, were not the manner of emotions she had earlier been referring to, she could nevertheless sense their overwhelming power.

And he was right, that power stirred alarm in her soul and set her heart beating to a fearful rhythm. For she knew she possessed no spiritual antidote that would give her the means or the will to resist it.

With a slow smile, he reached out and touched her hair, pushing the Titian curls softly back from her face, his dark eyes melting into hers as he told her, 'You're a very special girl, *habibiti*. Very special and very sweet.'

At the touch of his fingers, her heart skipped a beat and a delicious, warm sensation swept through her veins. Suddenly her nerve-ends were shimmering and dancing from her scalp right down to the soles of her feet.

'Giselle, Giselle . . . *Jamila* Giselle . . .'

As he leaned towards her she gasped in mute protest, one hand pressed to his chest to push him away. But as the touch of his fingers quickened in her hair, turning her spine to water and her blood to fire, somehow the push became a caress. And all she could do was sigh and surrender as his head bent closer and his mouth sought hers.

A moment later, as his arms closed round her, he was forcing her pliant lips to part, sending a shiver of longing writhing through her, threatening to tear her soul apart.

And she was drowning, drowning, listening to his heartbeat that thudded like a hammer beneath the palm of her hand, feeling the strength of the man and the strength of his passion taking hold of her and placing her at their command.

And she revelled in this new, wild sensation of surrender—both his surrender and her own. For this was no cold and calculated overture, like the encounters she had experienced with him in the past. This kiss that consumed her, this body that embraced her drew their passion and their power straight from his heart.

As her fingers trailed deliciously through his dark hair, revelling in the cool, soft, silky feel of it, suddenly he was drawing her back against the cushions, the warm weight of him pressing against her breasts. And she made not a single move to stop him as he began to undo the buttons of her dress.

As each one fell open, from neck to waist, he bent to kiss the newly exposed flesh, his lips sending hot and cold shivers through her, making her moan deep in her throat. Then she shuddered as he expertly reached behind her to undo the fastening of her white lacy bra.

'Giselle, *habibiti*, how splendid you are!' In one movement he had slipped both bra and dress from her shoulders, his eyes filled with a sweet and burning passion as his hands came round to claim her breasts.

His touch was firm and sure, an erotic delight, as he caressed the warm, excited flesh. Then, just as she thought she could bear no more pleasure, suddenly he was bending down hungrily to take one throbbing pink nipple into his mouth.

It was a sensation she had never before experienced. A sharp, indescribable burst of pure pleasure that arched her back and caused her to cry out as it shot through her nerve-ends like an explosion. Then her cry became a moan as his tongue circled wickedly, lazily tantalising the stiff, hard peak, then driving her wild as his lips grew more greedy, pulling hungrily on her achingly aroused flesh. With a cry of abandon she dug her fingers into his shoulders as hot longing, like a tidal wave, went sweeping through her loins.

As she pressed herself against him, shivering for him, longing for him, he moved lithely to cover her body with his, the warmth of his mouth once more claiming hers, his hands continuing where his lips had left off the subtle sweet torment of her breasts.

She could feel his male hardness press against her, announcing the rampant hunger in him, and as one hand slid down beneath the skirt of her dress to caress the bare trembling flesh of her abdomen, every agonised sinew in her body was crying out for him. Longing with an anguish that overwhelmed her for their two separate beings to fuse into one.

But suddenly Fayiz sighed and pressed his face against her, his warm, caressing fingers growing still as he whispered softly against her cheek, 'Time to call a halt, my sweet Giselle. Before we lose control completely.'

He lifted his tousled dark head to look at her, hot passion still burning from the coal-black eyes, and with the hint of a faintly self-mocking smile, dropped a warm, gentle kiss against her neck. 'I don't think this sofa was designed for such activities. We're liable to end up crashing to the floor!' Then as she smiled in response, he pulled a humorous face. 'And there's nothing more guaranteed to spoil the moment than a sudden, unscheduled descent!'

Giselle's poor throbbing heart was still pounding, but she managed to laugh gratefully all the same. He had transformed what could have been a supremely awkward moment into one that was warm and funny instead. She nuzzled her face gratefully against him as he held her close and kissed her again. For she knew he had been perfectly right to stop them. They had been heading at full throttle in a direction they both might ultimately have regretted.

Slipping her dress back round her shoulders to safeguard her modesty, Fayiz discreetly disengaged himself. 'Would you like a nightcap before you turn in? I'm going to have one. It'll help you to sleep.'

But as he helped her to her feet and she did up her buttons, Giselle felt it prudent to decline. 'No, thanks,' she told him. 'I'll just go straight to bed.'

His hand on her arm, he accompanied her to her bedroom and then, as though it was suddenly the most natural thing in the world, he was bending to kiss her a lingering goodnight.

'Sleep well, *habibiti*,' he exhorted her, letting his fingers delicately caress her cheek.

Then she was watching as he turned and strode off down the corridor, knowing only too well that she wouldn't sleep a wink.

She had been perfectly right. She didn't sleep. Not that night nor for several nights afterwards. For, suddenly, a thousand and one conflicting questions were thrumming feverishly inside her brain.

The first and biggest, the one she most feared, was: did she love Fayiz, after all?

It felt like love, this cruel and desperate longing she experienced now whenever he was near. All at once each glance in her direction caused her heart to dance and her blood to leap. She could not look at his face without remembering how delicious his lips had felt against her own, and her very soul burned with a dreadful, illogical anguish to imagine that they might never kiss her again.

For there had been no repetition of that evening in the drawing-room, no replay of the passion on the red damask sofa. For all the attention he had paid her since that evening, the entire deeply disruptive episode might have been a mere fleeting figment of her imagination.

He seemed distracted, she had thought as she watched him, surreptitiously, from the corner of her eye. But that was surely understandable. The battle over Rasha was preying on his mind. And perhaps too, she wondered, her heart clenching with optimism, he was examining more closely his feelings for her.

For she had not imagined the emotion she had felt in him as he had held her in his arms that night. Beyond the mere passion that had enthralled them she had sensed a deeper, more elemental bond. Though their bodies had resisted that ultimate union, she had felt their two spirits meld and unite. And he had felt it too. Of that she was certain. It had been too strong for the truth to be otherwise.

She continued to watch him, waiting, waiting, knowing that sooner or later he must come to her. Sooner or later, if she could just be patient, he would come and lay his heart before her. And then she would know, without reservation, what her answer to his proposal must be.

Her heart leapt at the thought and she thanked her good fortune that he had refused to take her initial answer. How unexpectedly situations could alter, and how deeply grateful she was for that.

But for the moment she must wait until he was ready. He would make his move soon enough.

* * *

She was right. He made his move just two days later.

There had been no dinner party that evening and Giselle had spent the evening in the flat alone. Just after eleven she switched off the television and decided to take herself off to bed. She was tired and tomorrow promised to be hectic. She would read for a while, then get her head down early for a change.

She was on her way down the corridor to her bedroom when she suddenly remembered the message for Fayiz. She had scribbled it on a piece of paper, intending to pass it on to him when he got back. But he hadn't returned yet, which posed something of a problem, for the caller had stressed that the message was urgent. She took the folded piece of paper from her pocket and decided to slip it beneath his bedroom door. That way he was bound to find it whenever he did eventually get back.

But as she turned the corner into the corridor, at the far end of which Fayiz's room was located, she was ever so slightly taken aback to see a light shining under his door. How strange, she reflected. I didn't hear him come in. Then, frowning a little, she tapped on the door.

There was no answer immediately and she was about to knock again when a gruff voice on the other side demanded, 'Who is it? What do you want?'

'It's me. Giselle.' She bent towards the door. 'I have an important message for you.'

There was another slight pause and then he commanded, 'OK, you'd better come in.'

He was seated behind the desk in the corner, she could see as she nervously pushed open the door. And it was piled with papers which he had obviously been working on, judging by the shirt sleeves pushed back to his elbows and the faintly dishevelled look of his hair.

'I'm sorry if I interrupted you,' her tone was apologetic, 'but Mr Mohammed al-Attiyah called you earlier. He wants you to call him back immediately. He said it was something rather urgent.' She took a step further into the room and held out the piece of paper towards him. 'He left his number, just in case you don't have it.'

Fayiz dismissed her overtures with a wave of his hand. 'I already spoke to him half an hour ago. You could have saved yourself the trouble.'

'I wish I had!' Giselle shot back tartly, as she turned on her heel and started to leave. Sometimes he had no manners at all, and, whether he knew it or not, he could be downright hurtful!

But she had got no further than a couple of steps when he was on his feet and striding up behind her. He caught hold of her arm and drew her back into the room, pointedly closing the door behind her. 'I'm sorry, I shouldn't have snapped at you like that. Come in and sit down. I've been wanting a chance to talk to you.'

Giselle's heart gave a little lift as he led her to a chair and, his hands on her arms, lowered her gently into it. Then, with an apologetic smile, he arranged another chair in front of her, sat down on it and leaned towards her. 'I've been pretty well snowed under with work these past few days. It seems to be making me bad-tempered.'

She smiled back at him, responding to his change of demeanour. 'I've told you before, you overdo it. You really ought to cut down, you know—for the sake of your health, if nothing else.'

He took her hand and raised it to his lips to bestow a soft and gentle kiss. 'You're a very sweet girl, Giselle,' he told her. 'And what's more, you're absolutely right. I ought to start thinking more about my health. I have Rasha's welfare to consider. I'm not going to be a great deal of good to her—or to anybody else, come to that—if I'm a clapped-out invalid before I'm forty.'

That was an image impossible to envisage. Somehow Giselle felt absolutely certain that the vital and vigorously male figure before her, whose very nearness was making her shiver, would never be anything other than superbly fit. But as she allowed herself a smile at his observation, she was aware of a warm glow in her heart. Could the 'anyone else' that he had just mentioned possibly be a sideways reference to her?

She smiled across at him, feeling her confidence growing. 'On the subject of Rasha, I've been wondering—has there been any progress regarding custody yet?'

He shook his head. 'It's early days yet. You know how slowly the law progresses. For the moment I guess I'll just have to be patient.'

'You'll win in the end, I'm perfectly sure of it. You and Rasha were meant to be together.'

'Let's hope you're right.' Fayiz smiled back gratefully. 'For us to be a family again, that's what I dream of.'

The warm glow in her heart grew a little stronger. 'A family,' he'd said. She had not imagined it. And suddenly she felt bold enough to ask him, 'You said you wanted to speak to me. What about?'

He had dropped her hand back into her lap, but he was still sitting so close to her, his legs spread apart, that her knees were almost touching the insides of his thighs. As he moved even closer to her before answering, so that the sudden swift touch of him sent shockwaves through her flesh, Giselle was suddenly burningly conscious of the context of the room that the two of them were sitting in.

Right behind her stretched his bed, a huge, silk-covered expanse of temptation. And suddenly in her mind's eye Giselle could envisage what a perfect setting it would provide for the celebration of their breathtakingly imminent betrothal. Fayiz had joked before of the inadequacy of the sofa as a platform for the physical expression of their love. This time there would be no such constraints upon them. This time they could allow themselves to be swept away in comfort in the ultimate fulfilment of their passion and their love.

At the thought her insides twisted wickedly. Had not even Gloria praised his talents as a lover? As he reached now to touch one hand lightly to her cheek, she shivered in burning anticipation. Oh, Fayiz, darling Fayiz, she begged him with her eyes. Don't make me wait any longer. Say it now.

'My sweet Giselle!' He was leaning towards her, his lips, soft as gossamer, brushing against hers. 'I've told you before, you're a very special girl. A very special girl indeed.'

Her heart was bursting as he leaned back a little and gazed into her face with those burning black eyes. And she could barely endure the suspense of waiting. 'Yes? Go on,' she prompted huskily.

With one finger he traced the line of her jaw, turning her limbs and her insides to jelly. 'But I haven't been fair to you, have I?' he murmured.

I forgive you, I forgive you, she answered soundlessly. Don't you know I would forgive you anything now?

He took her hand and held it lightly. 'So I've decided to do you a favour.' He paused a heartbeat, then continued, touching her fingers to his lips as he did so, 'I'm going to release you from your contract with me. As of this very moment you're free to go.'

Giselle's heart stopped dead. She stared at him blankly. 'I don't understand,' she croaked.

With a sigh he laid her numb hand back in her lap. 'I think it's for the best, and anyway, I've made up my mind. We're more or less at the end of the summer now, anyway. I'm sure I can find someone, though less able than yourself, to fill your shoes for the next few weeks.'

Giselle shook her head, feeling the nightmare

close round her. 'But I don't want——' she tried to interrupt.

He held up his hand before she could finish the sentence. 'I know you would have fulfilled your contract, whatever happened. But I have a feeling that things are going to get pretty nasty with Gloria over the next few weeks and I definitely don't want you getting dragged into that. I already feel badly enough, as it is, about the way she insulted you.'

'But that doesn't matter!'

'Oh yes, it does. I know the vicious power of Gloria's tongue, and believe me, you haven't heard anything yet! I know I would never forgive myself if she were to hurt or damage you in any way. That's why I can't let you stay on here.'

So he was sending her away. Her heart dropped to her shoes. 'It's not necessary—really. I assure you,' she stuttered.

'Oh, but it is, *jamila* Giselle.' His hand was on her cheek again, making her heart bleed. 'I want you to go back home to Honeybee Cottage, get on with your life and just forget all this.' He held her eyes for a heart-rending moment. '*All* of it, including my unforgivable proposal—for which I offer my sincere apologies. I had no right to do that. No right at all. Please forget it ever happened.'

She could not look at him. She stared at the floor.

'Will you do that for me? Please, Giselle,' he was saying.

She could not speak, yet somehow she forced herself. 'Yes. Yes, of course,' she said.

Fayiz had stood up and was reaching for his

discarded jacket, taking a folded piece of paper from the inside pocket. Standing over her, he held it out to her. 'The money I owe you, plus a small bonus. I hope it will enable you to restart Silver Service Catering.'

With a frozen heart, Giselle looked down at the piece of paper which he had somehow managed to slip into her hand. It was a cheque. Through blurred eyes, with an effort, she managed to read it, then she looked up at him, frowning. 'You don't owe me this much!' she protested.

His hand closed round hers, brooking no argument, as she màde a gesture to hand it back to him. 'Take it, *habibiti*. You've more than earned it. Take it—please. With my blessing.'

She took it. 'Thank you.' There was no point in arguing. Then she stuffed it into her pocket and rose shakily to her feet.

'So now,' Fayiz was saying, 'your purgatory is over. You are free to return to your old way of life and pick up where you left off.'

Giselle was only dimly aware of her answer. 'Thank you,' she was saying in a steady, controlled voice. 'I hope everything turns out right for you too.'

Then she was walking on very stiff legs, that felt as though they might fold beneath her, away from all she had learned to love and long for, towards a future that seemed endlessly bleak and empty.

CHAPTER TEN

FROM the top of the hill she could see the cathedral, ancient and gleaming in the late August sun. Giselle sighed and sank down on the warm, mossy grass, reflecting how cruel and fickle life could be. Here in Hereford, the home of her childhood, was the very last place she had expected to be.

The decision to return to the home of her parents, for an 'indefinite holiday', as she had told them, had been made with the sharp impetuosity of one who was torn apart with grief. Suddenly she could not bear to be alone down in Kent. In this her most cruel hour of darkness she needed the love and support of her family around her.

At first she had tried to cope alone. After leaving London, just two brief days after that fateful talk with Fayiz, and without setting eyes on him again, she had returned, full of bravery and good intentions, to Honeybee Cottage to set up business once again. Her temporary boarder, by a stroke of good fortune, had departed early for a holiday on the Continent, leaving her the cottage all to herself, and with the money from Fayiz she had more than enough to buy all the things that she would need. There was absolutely nothing stopping her from setting up Silver Service Catering again.

So she had spent hours scanning local newspaper ads for bargains in second-hand vans, and afternoons scanning the Yellow Pages for names of catering equipment suppliers. She had sat riffling diligently through the files of old clients, intending to ring them to say she was back, and she had rummaged assiduously through her piles of recipe books, searching for new dishes to add to her repertoire.

But that was precisely as far as she'd got. She had bought nothing in the end, neither van nor equipment. Nor had she phoned any of her old clients, nor bothered to try out a single new recipe. Somehow there didn't really seem much point. Nothing meant anything without Fayiz any more.

For a whole week Giselle had wallowed in her misery, pulling down the blinds and taking to her bed. Then, firmly, she had pulled herself up by her bootstraps. There was no point in agonising over a man who had never really wanted her and who would only despise her if he could see her now and accuse her of wallowing and snivelling like a child.

That accusation had snapped her to her senses once before and it had a similarly salutary effect this time around. With a sudden sense of duty to herself, she had started making some serious plans.

First, because she really did need a holiday and knew that a week or two with her family would be the best possible tonic, she had decided to take a break in Hereford. While she was there she would exorcise the ghost of Fayiz—a much easier task in those distant surroundings than at Honeybee Cottage, virtually in the shadow of Chiltham Hall. And then, when she was completely over him, she would head back to Kent again and get back into harness.

Her parents, as she had known they would be, were delighted to see her. 'Stay as long as you like, love,' her mother had urged her, settling her into her familiar old room. 'We don't see nearly enough of you these days. It'll be a regular treat having you around for a bit.'

'It'll be a treat being here,' Giselle had assured her, giving her mother a warm, loving hug. 'This is exactly what I need—a total change from everything.'

'There's nothing wrong, is there, Giselle?' For a moment her mother's expression puckered.

Giselle leaned and kissed her. 'Of course there isn't. I just need a bit of a change of scenery, that's all.'

And she had come to exactly the right place for that, she soon discovered as the days sped past. The hilly countryside, right on the Welsh border, where almost daily she went for long walks, could scarcely have been more different from the softly rolling contours of Kent. And it was good and relaxing to spend a lazy Sunday picnicking with her parents on the banks of the River Wye, and to catch up later with some old friends at a wine bar and reminisce about their schooldays together.

It was all like another world entirely. A million

light years away from Fayiz and Belgravia.

And, with each day that passed, she was feeling stronger. The ache inside her had subsided sufficiently to allow her to take a closer look at it.

It would almost certainly never entirely vanish, she decided, as she sat quietly now on the hillside. It would always be there as a cruel reminder of the bitter folly of misguided love. For no love, surely, in the history of the universe had been more misguided than her love for Fayiz. Doomed even before it had been begotten, its only purpose had been to bring her pain.

With a sigh she rested her chin on her knees and circled her trouser-clad legs with her arms. Perhaps it would be better if she had never met him, never known him and grown so hopelessly to love him, never been beckoned into his world only to be forced back out of it again.

But she thrust the thought from her, knowing it to be unworthy. She would not be bitter. It was foolish to regret. Instead, she would be grateful for what he had given her—a fresh and totally new perspective on life, much broader and more open than before. Not to mention, of course, she thought with a wry smile, the iron he had injected into her soul. She would never again let life trample all over her. Her days of snivelling and wallowing were over. From now on, like him, she would be a survivor.

She smiled to herself as she gazed down at the cathedral. Her next step was to prove that she really meant it. Flexing her shoulders, she rose to her feet and, with a last long look out over the countryside, began the long trek back down the hill to her parents' home on the outskirts of the town. Tonight at dinner she would tell them she was leaving. Then tomorrow she would return to Kent and pick up the threads of her life again.

She was halfway up the path to her parents' little bungalow when she had her first inclination that something was amiss. And as she pushed open the back door into the kitchen she could definitely tell there was something going on.

Her mother was arranging some things on a tea-tray—her very best china, no less, Giselle observed. And her habitually calm and good-natured face was alight with a mixture of mild panic and delight, as though the Queen herself had just dropped in for tea.

At the sight of her daughter she literally jumped. 'Oh, there you are, my girl! At last!' she exclaimed.

Giselle was frowning. 'What on earth's up, Mum? Have we got visitors? Let me give you a hand.'

But her mother waved her impatiently away. 'I can manage perfectly, thank you.' Then she paused to look her up and down, her eyes openly condemning the plain trousers and T-shirt. 'Hurry on through to your room and get changed. You can't possibly meet him looking like that!'

Giselle frowned harder. 'What are you talking about? Who can't I meet? What's going on?'

'Just do as I say! Don't ask so many questions! Go on, my girl, hurry up and——'

But even as she began shooing her bewildered daughter in the direction of the corridor that led to the bedrooms, she stopped abruptly in mid-sentence, blushing to the roots of her hair. With a stab of mild anxiety at her stricken expression Giselle snapped round to follow her mother's gaze.

For an instant shock rooted her to the spot. She could feel prickles on her scalp and numbness in her toes. For standing there in the doorway to the sitting-room, looking as unlikely as a visitor from another planet, was a tall, familiar figure in a dark grey suit.

Their eyes met and held, then he was stepping towards her. 'Hello, Giselle. Surprised to see me?'

Aghast, not surprised! She could not believe it! Even the sound of his voice had failed entirely to convince her that the sight she beheld was not some kind of mirage. Any minute now she would hear the buzz of her alarm clock and know for certain that this was all a dream.

But then he reached out to touch her and it felt like bright sunlight gently caressing the skin of her arm. With an effort of will she managed to speak. 'Fayiz. What are you doing here?'

'I could always say that I just happened to be passing, but I'm afraid that that would be a lie.' Though there was a smile in his voice, the dark eyes were serious and the fingers around her arm were firm. 'The truth is I've come to see you, *habibiti*. If you'll allow it, I'd like for us to have a little talk.'

Without waiting for her answer, he glanced

across at her mother, who was watching the scene with a barely suppressed smile. 'Is there somewhere private we could go, Mrs Copeland? Somewhere where we won't be in your way?'

Giselle's mother, quite clearly, was a more than willing ally. 'The back garden's the best place—it's nice and secluded. There are some garden seats and things down at the bottom. Giselle will show you where.'

Fayiz nodded. 'Thanks,' he acknowledged. Then he was propelling a dazed and bewildered Giselle out into the garden and down beyond the chestnut tree to the little hedged-in area at the bottom where some white-painted benches and a table were arranged. He glanced around him. 'This is perfect.'

'Perfect for what, I'd like to know?' Now that they were private Giselle gave vent to her annoyance that had been building up with a vengeance on the short journey across the garden. 'What business do you think you have coming here, just barging in and taking over? I don't know what you want to talk to me about, but it was arrogant of you in the extreme to descend on my parents' home in order to do it!'

He was standing before her, very still, and so desperately handsome it took her breath away. She had forgotten how perfect were the lines of his nose, the wide passionate mouth, the smooth high brow. And she had forgotten, too, perhaps for self-protection, the impossible blackness of those deep velvet eyes.

Beneath the dark jacket he was wearing his

customary white shirt, crisp and bright against the dark sheen of his hair, and the blue and grey striped tie at his throat, ever so slightly askew, she imagined, made her nerveless fingers burn with the desire to reach up and lovingly set it straight.

But she kept her hands clenched tightly at her sides and deliberately whipped up the anger inside her. Anger and resentment and a bitter sense of helplessness that seemed to grow with every aching heartbeat. Just in a matter of a couple of minutes he had undone all her good work of the past two and a half weeks.

Keeping a grip on her emotions, Giselle demanded tightly, 'You'd better tell me, then. What have you come for?'

'I told you, *habibiti*. I came to see you.'

'Couldn't you have waited till I got back to Kent?'

'I waited. You did not come.'

'All you had to do was wait another day. I was planning to return tomorrow.'

His lips pursed slightly. 'I had no way of knowing. For all I knew, you might have stayed away forever.'

Was it purely her imagination or had there been a slight inflection in his voice as he had said that about her staying away forever, almost as though such a prospect pained him? The suspicion sent a flutter through her heart. She demanded prosaically, 'How did you find me?'

'Easy.' She felt him smile down at her wryly. 'I simply phoned up every Copeland in the Hereford phone book until I finally hit on the right one.'

'You spoke to my parents?' Her eyes snapped angrily. 'How dare you? What did you say to them?'

'I spoke to your father. I told him I was a friend and that I was thinking of looking you up. I also told him that I wanted to surprise you and made him promise not to say a word.'

How very typical! 'I see you haven't changed! Still as devious and manipulative as ever!'

Fayiz shook his head and this time, definitely, there was an unmistakable catch in his voice as he answered, 'People don't change much in two and a half weeks. At least——' he paused '——not as a rule.' Then his hands were on her arms and he was drawing her down gently to sit on one of the white-painted benches. He sat down next to her and turned towards her with an earnest frown shadowing his face. 'That's really what I want to talk to you about. About changes. What you might call changes of the heart.'

Giselle had told herself that he was here on business, something to do with her Belgravia contract. In as much as she was capable of thinking at all, it had seemed the safest, most sensible thing to think. Now, suddenly, as she caught the tension in his face, the unaccustomed hesitancy in his manner, a wave of anxiety rose up inside her.

Whose heart was he talking about? What were the changes he had alluded to? Suddenly, as she grappled with those unanswered questions, her anxiety turned to ice-cold fear.

It was the fear of hoping, of daring to dream that there might be something worth hoping for. And the dreadful fear, even as hope wanly flickered, that all that waited in the wings was more pain.

She looked at him levelly, almost threateningly, as though warding off the threat he posed her. 'Changes?' she repeated. 'What sort of changes?' Then she added quickly, before he could answer, 'Something to do with Rasha, no doubt?'

Fayiz paused, then to her dismay he nodded. 'Yes, there have been changes there. According to my solicitor—and Gloria's—it seems certain now that I shall have custody.'

'That's wonderful news!' With all her heart she meant it, though it was far from being the news she had been secretly praying for. She kept her voice steady, almost distant. 'So how did that state of affairs come about?'

'Mainly thanks to my devious nature.' Fayiz paused and smiled a gentle smile. Then his expression momentarily hardened as he went on to elaborate, 'Through my spies I managed to discover that my even more devious and greedy ex-wife was planning to spirit Rasha off to Rio—but only after relieving me of a large sum of money.'

He shook his head. 'Soon after you left, after a bit of a wrangle, she told me she would be prepared to surrender custody if I paid her a lump sum in compensation. I hated the idea of having to buy back my daughter, but if all else had failed I would have agreed to it. Luckily, however, I uncovered the truth before I lost both my money and my daughter.

'It transpires that Gloria is soon to be married, to a fellow Brazilian based in Rio. However, sadly for Gloria, though he's far from penniless, this man who is soon to be her husband is not in the financial bracket to which she has become accustomed. Hence her demand for a large sum of money in exchange for the custody rights of our daughter.

'However——' he paused for a moment, his expression sharpening '—the lovely Gloria had devised a plan to pocket the money and then, before anyone could stop her, disappear off with Rasha to Brazil, thus scoring the double victory of fleecing me of a considerable sum of money and at the same time robbing me of my daughter.' The fine lips curled in a show of distaste. 'Even she, I had not believed, could sink so low.'

Giselle, personally, had no trouble at all in believing such a thing. 'I'm glad you managed to stop her in time. So what happened in the end?'

'Well, there was quite a rumpus when it was discovered that she was planning on taking Rasha to Rio. The conditions of the custody order stipulated that Rasha must remain in this country, unless special permission was granted for her to be removed. Permission which had to be agreed by me—and which Gloria knew I would never agree to. So, in the end, without making a single penny out of it, she was forced, by law, to relinquish custody to me. It was either that or abandon her plans for remarriage. In the event it took her no time at all to decide.'

It was a happy ending to a long and troubled story. 'I'm pleased for you,' Giselle told him. 'Really pleased. I'm sure you and Rasha will both be very happy.'

'That's what I thought too. But there was something missing.' Suddenly he was leaning towards her again and reaching across to take hold of her hand. Giselle scarcely dared breathe as he went on to tell her, 'As soon as I got the news that the fight was finally over, I realised I still had a major problem.' His eyes held hers, intent and darkly probing. 'I was desperately longing to share my good news, and I suddenly realised I had no one to share it with.'

'You could have phoned someone. Anyone. A friend.'

'That's not what I mean. I mean someone special.' He grasped her hand firmly. 'Giselle, I mean you.'

In the silence that followed her heart had stopped beating. Her eyes dared not focus on his face. 'Me?' she said stupidly. 'You could have phoned me if you'd wanted. I wouldn't have minded in the least.'

'Oh, *habibiti, habibiti*! You misunderstand me.' Fayiz had risen now and was drawing her to her feet. 'I didn't want to phone you. I wanted you there. I wanted you there as part of my life.' One strong arm was round her, holding her to him, while his other hand gently tilted her face. He looked into her eyes a long, endless moment, drawing her into the sweet warm caverns of his soul. 'I love you,

Giselle. I want to marry you. I want us never to be apart again.'

As she hesitated, not daring to believe what she was hearing, her heart torn asunder by the emotions that ripped through her, he drew her to him and kissed her gently, murmuring softly through her hair, 'Forget that previous offer of marriage. It was a cynical gesture, which you rightly rejected and for which, again, I beg you to forgive me. As you insisted then, there must be love in marriage. Marriage is nothing without love.' He drew her back a little, her head held in his hands. 'In truth, I think I loved you from the beginning, but I was reluctant to admit it, even to myself. I had sworn I would never again fall prey to a woman, and I allowed that foolish determination to blind me.'

He kissed her softly. 'Can you forgive me? For my blindness and for my foolish fears? After the débâcle of my marriage I was literally terrified of making the same mistake again. That, dear Giselle, is the true reason that I decided to keep my feelings under lock and key. I thought it might be possible to live my life without them—but, thanks to you, I discovered I was wrong.'

He smoothed her hair, holding her tightly as he continued, 'When I sent you away, it was for many, many reasons, not just the reason I gave. Sure, I was worried that Gloria might upset you, but I was really more troubled by my feelings for you. You see, I hadn't been prepared for what was happening to me. I was starting to feel that I needed you. That was why I had to send you away, so that I could sort those feelings out.' He sighed and let his eyes melt into hers. 'Can you understand, and forgive?' he asked.

Giselle nodded, her heart filled with overwhelming love for him. 'I understand and I forgive,' she said.

Momentarily his expression lightened. He hugged her to him and then he frowned again. 'Now there remains but one question to be answered—do you love me as I love you?'

She gazed into his face. 'How do you love me?'

'With all my heart. As I have never loved before.'

And his heart was in his eyes, naked and raw. She could see for herself the love that shone there. As she answered, her own poor heart was bursting. 'Then my answer is yes. For that's how I love you.'

'Giselle, *habibiti* . . .!'

The words were a prayer. A prayer of thanks and adoration. With a sigh he gathered her into his arms.

'Come to me. Be with me forever!'

'Go on . . . you choose, Fayiz. Which shall we have? The clouds or the flowers?'

'This one.' Without a moment's hesitation he flicked through the pages of wallpaper samples and pointed to the one with the blue and white clouds. He threw a teasing smile across at her. 'I think it's more suitable for a boy.'

She had known he would say that and she prodded him playfully. 'What makes you so sure it's going to be a boy?'

'An instinct. Masculine intuition. Besides, Rasha has told you she wants a little brother.' He picked up the book of samples from the bed and dropped it with a small thud on to the floor. Then, pushing back the pillows at their heads, he drew Giselle into his arms. 'And if we're wrong it doesn't really matter. We'll simply pull the clouds down and put up flowers instead.' He kissed her brow, his lips warm and lingering. 'All that matters is that you and I are together.'

With a sigh Giselle rested her cheek against his chest, feeling his heartbeat strong and sure and steady. Already she felt almost as though they had been together forever, as though all that had passed before had been a dream. She reached up and kissed the warm pulse of his throat. Was it really possible for two people to be this happy?

That afternoon in the garden up in Hereford had marked the true beginning of their brand new life. A life of no more fears or misunderstandings. The life of two hearts bound together with love.

Giselle still remembered her mother's expression when they had walked back into the kitchen, hand in hand, and announced their intention soon to marry. She had taken both of them in her arms and hugged them fiercely, then promptly burst into floods of tears. And later, in private, she had told her daughter, 'I knew all along there was something troubling you, some secret sadness in your heart. As soon as I saw Fayiz I knew he was behind it—and I was certain, too, that all your troubles were over.' She had drawn Giselle into her arms and kissed her. 'Your father and I just couldn't be happier. We wish you both a lifetime of love.'

That unquestioning delight in the forthcoming union had been echoed in turn by little Rasha. On the very day that Fayiz's custody rights were granted, together they had broken the happy news to her.

'Does that mean that the three of us can live together?' she had demanded to know, her eyes bright with delight. And as her father nodded, she had grinned and whooped gleefully. 'I think that's going to be the bestest!' she proclaimed.

The wedding took place a week to the day after Rasha was installed officially in the penthouse in Belgravia. And it was a truly sumptuous affair with the reception held in a huge marquee in the grounds of Chiltham Hall. Then had followed a dream honeymoon in the Bahamas—three whole weeks of heaven on earth. And it was there, beneath the warm, cloudless skies of Nassau, that the child Giselle now carried had been conceived.

She glanced up now at Fayiz as he stirred and kissed her, sending warm, sensuous ripples over her skin. It was a sunny Sunday afternoon and a warm golden autumn light filled the room. All around them throughout the country people were having a lazy day doing nothing, and it felt good to be among them.

Not that it was particularly unusual these days for Fayiz to take the weekend off. It was a habit he was fast acquiring, along with an equally pleasing tendency to finish work no later than six o'clock.

'You may live to regret it,' he had teased her, when she had pointed out this happy and flattering change in him. 'You'll get so sick of having me kicking about your feet you'll soon be packing me off back to the office again!'

Some chance! she thought now with a tender smile, as he drew her softly to him and kissed her. She could never have enough of this wonderful man, if she had him to herself twenty-four hours a day! In the past few weeks he had made her feel more loved than she had ever believed it possible to feel. Of one thing she was certain: no man in the world had ever made a woman more deeply happy.

He was stroking her cheek. 'What are you thinking about?'

She kissed him warmly. 'I was thinking that I love you.'

'Then tell me, *habibiti*. Don't keep it to yourself.'

'But I've told you a thousand times,' she protested, smiling, her skin shivering beneath his touch as he caressed her.

'Tell me a thousand times more, and a thousand more after that. Don't you know how greedy I am for your love?'

'And I for yours.' She pressed against him, her body thrilling as she felt him stir against her.

'Then you shall have it.' His lips covered hers, consuming her with a kiss alight with passion and love. 'But first you must tell me again that you love me.'

Coming soon
to an easy chair near you.

FIRST CLASS is Harlequin's armchair travel plan for the incurably romantic. You'll visit a different dreamy destination every month from January through December without ever packing a bag. No jet lag, no expensive air fares and *no* lost luggage. Just First Class Harlequin Romance reading, featuring exotic settings from Tasmania to Thailand, from Egypt to Australia, and more.

FIRST CLASS romantic excursions guaranteed! Start your world tour in January. Look for the special **FIRST CLASS** destination on selected Harlequin Romance titles—there's a new one every month.

NEXT DESTINATION:
GREECE

 Harlequin Books

JTR4

'I love you.' She kissed him back, equally fiercely, and circled his precious head with her arms. 'Always, *habibi*. Until I die.'

COMING IN 1991 FROM
HARLEQUIN SUPERROMANCE:

Three abandoned orphans,
one missing heiress!

Dying millionaire Owen Byrnside receives an
anonymous letter informing him that twenty-six years
ago, his son, Christopher, fathered a daughter. The
infant was abandoned at a foundling home that
subsequently burned to the ground, destroying all
records. Three young women could be Owen's long-
lost granddaughter, and Owen is determined to track
down each of them! Read their stories in

#434 HIGH STAKES (available January 1991)
#438 DARK WATERS (available February 1991)
#442 BRIGHT SECRETS (available March 1991)

Three exciting stories of intrigue and romance by
veteran Superromance author Jane Silverwood.

You'll flip . . . your pages won't!
Read paperbacks *hands-free* with

Book Mate·I

The perfect "mate" for all your romance paperbacks
**Traveling • Vacationing • At Work • In Bed • Studying
• Cooking • Eating**

Perfect size for all standard paperbacks, this wonderful invention makes reading a pure pleasure! Ingenious design holds paperback books OPEN and FLAT so even wind can't ruffle pages – leaves your hands free to do other things. Reinforced, wipe-clean vinyl-covered holder flexes to let you turn pages without undoing the strap . . . supports paperbacks so well, they have the strength of hardcovers!

Pages turn WITHOUT opening the strap

SEE-THROUGH STRAP

Reinforced back stays flat

Built in bookmark

BOOK MARK

BACK COVER
HOLDING STRIP

10˝ x 7¼˝ . opened.
Snaps closed for easy carrying, too

Available now. Send your name, address, and zip code, along with a check or money order for just $5.95 + .75¢ for delivery (for a total of $6.70) payable to Reader Service to:

Reader Service
Bookmate Offer
3010 Walden Avenue
P.O. Box 1396
Buffalo, N.Y. 14269-1396

Offer not available in Canada
*New York residents add appropriate sales tax.

BM-GR

Harlequin Intrigue®

A SPAULDING & DARIEN MYSTERY
by Robin Francis

An engaging pair of amateur sleuths—Jenny Spaulding and Peter Darien—were introduced to Harlequin Intrigue readers in #147, BUTTON, BUTTON (Oct. 1990). Jenny and Peter will return for further spine-chilling romantic adventures in April 1991 in #159, DOUBLE DARE in which they solve their next puzzling mystery. Two other books featuring Jenny and Peter will follow in the A SPAULDING AND DARIEN MYSTERY series.

If you missed the debut of this exciting pair of sleuths and would like to order #147 BUTTON, BUTTON, send your name, address, zip or postal code along with a check or money order for $2.50 plus 75¢ postage and handling ($1.00 in Canada) for each book order, payable to Harlequin Reader Service, to:

In the U.S.
3010 Walden Ave.
P.O. Box 1325
Buffalo, NY 14269-1326

In Canada
P.O. Box 609
Fort Erie, Ontario
L2A 5X3

Canadian residents add applicable federal and provincial taxes.

IBB-1A

HARLEQUIN
Romance®

Coming Next Month

Available in April wherever paperback books are sold, or through
Harlequin Reader Service:

In the U.S.
P.O. Box 1397
Buffalo, N.Y.
14240-1397

In Canada
P.O. Box 603
Fort Erie, Ontario
L2A 5X3